THE FRIAR

THE FRIAR

MICHAEL DION

Other Books:

Circle of Chance

The Music Disc Murder

Saratoga Springs

Music is Life... and Death

ITI Music Corporation Publishing
16057 Tampa Palms Bl West
Tampa, FL 33543

RE-1

Registered with Library of Congress

ISBN: 978-0-9995684-7-7

Printed and bound in the United States

Cover: RoxC LLC/www.roxc.graphics/Roxanne Clapp

Author Photo: Ying/Rick Steves Tour 2018

Cover Photo: Michael Dion / The Church of San Giacometto 2018/Venice

To My Wife, Laura, every year brings new challenges, dreams, and hopes. But we are still together. Thank You. Much Love to you as we continue down this path.

To our Daughter and Family, we love you dearly.

I wish to thank my family and friends for continuing to support my efforts. Hopefully, those who do read my penned works will enjoy them as much as I have in creating them.

The Friar
Chapter One

Kneeling in prayer with the other five monks, the 23-year-old Friar, Niccolo Viteli from Monaco, sang as beautiful and as loud as the eldest of the Roman born priests in the Church of The Basilica of St. Clemente on the first of June.

According to the legends, it was St Cyril who was a Slav that brought Catholic relics to this Church in 869. However, the site dates back further to early Roman and pre-Christian days when it was a Mithraic Temple.

Mithraism was an all-male cult, that was imported from Persia during the first century BCE. It is said that this practice rivaled Christianity in the course of those days.

Almost nine hundred years later, the Temple part of the Church was now four layers below, while a daily mass was performed above, at street level.

On this warm day, disturbing the young Friar was an out of breath altar boy by the name of Giancarlo. Niccolo tried to ignore the boy with a look that said, "wait a minute," as the sweat trickled down his back as he knelt in deep-rooted prayer and song in the 12th century Church.

Customarily stationed at the Vatican, Giancarlo was tugging hard at the Friar's sleeve, and annoying the rest of the clergy in prayers.

Extremely disturbed, Niccolo stopped singing and walked the boy out into the courtyard that contained vegetables, fruits, and flowers.

There in the fragrant garden of the Church, the boy blurted out in Italian, "Mi scusi, Poppa Papal needs your help in a delicate matter, and since you have helped him in the past, he requires your immediate attention. Mi capisci?" (Do you understand me).

Puzzled, Niccolo replied, "Si, si. When does he need me to come to his aid?"

"Right away, Signore, Pronto pronto."

"Okay, but first, I must tell the Priory Priest, Father DiMarco. Wait for me," said the Friar.

After gathering a few items from his room, Niccolo and Giancarlo walked out the door, entering the street. They strode as fast as they could on the cobblestones, passing by the hamlet to the dirt road leading to the Vatican.

It took over an hour to reach the massive building off the side of Piazza San Pietro (St. Peter's Square).

Gian Lorenzo Bernini redesigned the open space between 1656 to 1667.

Pope Alexander VII directed it to allow for the most significant number of people to see the Pope give his blessing. It was to house up to 300,000 people.

Upon entering the edifice of the Vatican, the Swiss guards protecting the entrance recognized the boy and the Friar.

Niccolo was dressed in his summer linen robe of light brown that was now covered in dust and mud stains from the recent rain.

Smiling, the guards greeted the two with "Buona Giornata" and allowed them to pass since they were frequent visitors to the Pope's quarters.

Niccolo waved and responded, "Grazie Fabio and Ottavio."

Up the 53 steps of the staircase, the two climbed quickly and were out of breath, finally reaching the door of the Papal chamber. Bursting in, they were stopped momentarily by the secretary of the Pope, Cardinal Moriggia.

The Pope looking up, saw the two young men sweating profusely, and yelled out, "Attentzione."

Then Niccolo and Giancarlo walked up to the significant, ornate metal and wood writing desk where the Pope sat reading and signing papers.

Now looking at them he grinned and stood up.

Then the Pontiff reached inside a small-jeweled box on the table and collected a few coins and walked to Giancarlo.

Facing the boy, he extended his hand to drop the money into the youngster's hands.

The boy grasping the coins in his palms repeated, "Grazie, Grazie Poppa," and then withdrew from the room, leaving the Friar by himself.

"Holy Father, good day. I am here for your task. What may I do for you?"

The Pope grinned and thanked Niccolo for being so prompt then said, "Son, one of the Holiest of Holy relics has been taken from The Church. We think it might be the doings of the French Sun

King, Louis XIV, but we are not sure, so we need your expertise to find and return it at all costs."

In just ten years, there had been three Popes, Alexander VIII, Innocent XII, and now Clement. Each of them had to play a constant game of chess with the Kings and Queens of Europe.

When Pope Clement XI became the Head of the Church in November 1700, following Innocent's death, this accusation of Louis became the first real challenge of his young Papacy.

Clement was born in 1649, where he lived in a small hillside town on the Adriatic side.

He was raised in a well-off family with strong ancient ties to various noble families.

During his time as Pope, Clement would try to rectify the policy of Nepotism that had been prevalent throughout the ages of the Papacy, fighting long and hard battles with Cardinals and Kings alike.

Niccolo strained his thoughts to understand what could have been stolen, but came up with many possible relics?

Turning his thoughts to the past, the last time Clement needed him was for a missing vestment of Cardinal Magnani.

The Cardinal was about to be canonized but was stripped of it after findings of simony and other church dealings of fraud that surrounded Magnani.

Though Niccolo was able to retrieve the garment, it was later thrown into one of the Vatican's fireplaces, as it was no longer considered a sacred relic.

Now, The Pope was extremely sad and lamented what he had to do.

Sitting down in his decorative chair in the corner of his chamber, which was beside the window facing St Peter's Square, The Pope told the Friar the devastating news.

"From the Roman Catholic Church at San Silvestre in Capite, (Church of Pope Saint Sylvester the First), the skull of St. John the Baptist has been stolen. Granted, other churches throughout France, Germany, and Syria all claim to have the Head, however it's this relic that gives the Church its greatest reputation."

The Pope continued, "Originally built on top of pagan ruins (like many other Catholic Churches and other important buildings) to house relics of Saints and martyrs in the 8th Century, Pope Sylvester was canonized and was assigned to the newly rebuilt church."

Clement was almost crying in his explanation to the Friar.

Niccolo was stunned by the Pope's reaction to this robbery. However, Clement was such a religious person that any missing artifacts or relics from the Church were a vast heartbreak for His Holiness.

The Friar
Chapter Two

Unlike Clement, the Friar had been born in Monaco near the palace on La Rocher in a back alley.

His family worked for the royal house of Grimaldi and was considered a Monegasque who had exclusive rights and privileges. (A Monegasque is one who speaks a form of Gallo-Italic language).

As the first male child, he was designated to be a monk. But Niccolo opted to become a Friar instead, to assist the poor and needy.

During this time, Medieval cleric standings were as follows:

An Oblate was when parents gave a child to a monastic community to be raised as a monk.

A Postulant was an adult who sought to follow a religious order like a monk.

A Novice was one that was under training within a monastic community.

Growing up, Niccolo became an Oblate who was given up to the local monastery and where he learned to be an excellent sleuth for the monks and the Priory Priest.

The young Friar had a knack that even the local Bishop thought was miraculous. So, the Bishop would offer Niccolo's services to anyone looking for missing articles.

Hence, when the Genoese family needed someone who could recover a lost item, they employed the young religious lad in secret and covert situations that eventually led him to the Papal House.

The royal family of Monaco was otherwise known as the Grimaldi Dynasty. It originated in Italy and was founded by the Genoese leader, Francesco Grimaldi, who in 1297, with his soldiers dressed as monks took over the city.

So, in unusual and significant times of need, Niccolo was called into action. But after each case, he was sent back to his humble life as an Oblate. This occurred over and over again until the Vatican heard of his unique talent and requested his presence.

Approved by Clement, Niccolo became a Friar instead of a monk, so that he was free to travel wherever and whenever the Pope needed him.

Now listening to the Holy Father about St. John's Head, Niccolo asked, "Poppa, how am I to proceed?"

The Pope replied, "Niccolo, go about it in any way you see fit, and the Vatican will pay for and reimburse you for any additional expenses you might incur."

As the Friar turned to leave, the Pope's secretary handed Niccolo a bag full of gold that equated to 3000 lire.

The Friar then kissed the Pope's hand, who blessed the young man and wished him well in his findings.

Walking back by himself to the refectory, Niccolo devised his idea of a plan that would allow him access to the courts, palaces, and everyday locations of the ordinary people.

The Friar would present himself as a theology scholar on a mission to review artifacts for a private owner, located in Florence.

Since he had been given such a large sum of money, he would dress in the most elegant garments that could be purchased and spend the lire wherever he thought was necessary.

Though not a typical visitor to brothels and drinking establishments, he did not rule out the prospect of laying a trap in those places to locate missing relics.

He might be fortunate enough to find those everyday folks and or officials who may have deceived the Church and would speak freely to a "gentleman," thereby locating the stolen Head.

After explaining his Papal mission to Father DiMarco of St. Clémente's, he was given his leave and off to the garment maker and tailor he went.

Based on the information the Holy Father gave him, which was not much, Niccolo decided first to establish himself someplace close to the Legates of Spain, France, and Italy, in Rome.

From the Pope's secretary, he was able to locate such a place called "Roberto's Inn."

It would be there that he might find a lead where the sacred skull might be or who may have stolen St. John's Head.

The Friar
Chapter Three

The 14th century-built village of Orvieto, in Umbria, is a hill town that had existed since the time of the Etruscans. The early settlers were there between the 8th and 3rd centuries BCE.

However, in this little town, where most of the wine for the Central part of the region, including the Vatican was made, three farm workers: Matteo, Geovanni, and Alessio, were picking grapes and discovered a skull in one of their master's vineyard.

At first, they eyed it cautiously, then each one held it and spoke to the others about the uniqueness of it.

Matteo was the first to speak. "Hey, have you ever seen a skull before? It's ugly, yes?"

Alessio answered. "Yes, but I am sure that yours is every bit as this! After all, the falling down on the job you have done."

All three men laughed, but Geovanni said, "Suppose it's possessed and has powers that we do not know about? We should leave it alone and tell Dominic."

Matteo laughed and said, "Sure, but let's grab some sticks and kick it around first?"

Geovanni yelled, "No. I am not kidding. This could be an evil head from some witch!"

"Alright," replied Alessio, but then they went ahead and scared each other about tales of the devil and what the skull represented.

After a short while, they placed the skull alongside the outermost edge of the vineyard, for fear it might frighten anyone else who was working.

Finishing their jobs for the day, they did not tell the owner but agreed to discuss it later that night when they would meet at the local tavern.

Following his dinner, Alessio, who was laughing and playing with his kids at the table, stood up to leave and fell onto the earthen floor and died in front of his family.

His poor wife had no idea what happened or why since he was still a young man of only thirty-two years of age. She was mortified and cried so loud that her neighbors from down the road came running to her house.

Not aware of what had occurred to his young friend, Matteo, the eldest of the three men at forty-five though he looked like he was sixty-five, started walking on the road to the tavern when he fell over and died instantly.

The final worker, Geovanni, who was only forty, lived close to Alessio and Matteo and was asked by a cousin to go to the house where the young man's wife was in despair over his death. He had no idea that it was Alessio who had died.

As he started on the road to Alessio's house, he stumbled upon the body of Matteo and was now deeply troubled and scared for his own life.

"What had they found, smelled, and touched that would have such a drastic effect on their lives?", Geovanni asked himself.

"Should he tell someone about the skull they found and where it was placed?" he continued with his thoughts.

After consoling Alessio's family and perplexed by the events, Geovanni decided to return home and tell his wife. With only about 20 yards from his front door, Geovanni dropped to his knees, sighed, and then died in the road.

The following day their deaths caused alarm throughout the town.

Fear that the plague had returned seemed to spread throughout the area.

With the help of a few farmers with bibs and gloves on, they collected the bodies of all three men.

Placing them in a cart, they drove to a makeshift medical table that had been constructed outside.

There the doctor looked for evidence that might have caused their deaths.

The doctor and the local Priest, Father Nardella, searched their bodies to determine the reason behind their unlikely deaths, since there was no blackening of the men's lips or tongues or infections that they could find.

Agreeing with each other as to what they should do next, the Priest and doctor decided to gather the town's people together.

The Priest asked one of the altar boys, Enzo, to ring the Duomo chapel bell for the town meeting.

Father Nardella spoke first. He said, "People of my congregation. I call you together today to tell you what we do know of these tragic deaths."

Then Dr. Perna spoke and said, "Please be patient with our findings and do not panic. There is no evidence of the plague. But I will go to Rome to seek out other guidance concerning their deaths."

After reassuring the locals again, that it was not the plague, the village Priest asked the doctor to inform the magistrate in Rome of what had happened.

Perna said to the Priest, "It will take a minimum of two hours for me to reach the Papal City. In the meantime, my assistant, Paolo, would be in charge until I return."

That afternoon, the owner of the vineyards told his son Aldo to go out into the fields and look for anything questionable. His main concern was the loss of revenue if anything was wrong with his crops.

Dominic told his son, "If you find anything, bring it to me!"

"But Papa, what if it is the plague or something much more terrible," his son asked.

"Son, I think if it were such a terrible thing, then all of us would be died by now," Dominic replied.

It wasn't but a half an hour later when his son came running back towards the house, rushing through the doors to inform his father that he found a Head laying at the far end of the farm, but didn't touch it for fear of something dreadful would befall all of them.

Dominic, with Aldo in tow, went out to speak with the rest of his workers. He asked, "Has anyone seen anything suspicious? Apparently, there is a skull in our vineyard."

No one seemed to know anything about it, so Dominic, wanting it gone, had his son fetch the doctor.

However, upon arrival at the farm, Paolo said to the owner, "Dominic, as you may know, the doctor has gone to Rome to get help concerning the deaths of your men. So, I am not sure what else I can do?"

"Paolo, I need a skull removed from my property, so my workers will go back into the fields and harvest the grapes. Without that, the town and the Vatican will be without wine this year, and I can't afford to lose the money."

Agreeing with Dominic, the doctor's assistant and Aldo went to the spot where the skull had been placed.

As he eyed it from a short distance, Paolo said to Aldo, "There is nothing weird with this Head that I can tell." But he put gloves on for precaution, anyway.

Then the assistant wrapped the skull tightly with a cloth and placed it into the woolen bag.

Looking at Aldo, he said, "Will you help me carry this back to my office?"

Aldo replied, "Do you think it is safe?"

Paolo smiled and said, "Yes, I have seen many in my training at La Sapienza in Rome. And I have taken several apart and glued them back together, like a puzzle."

The two men grinned at one another and placed the skull between the wooden kegs in the cart, securing it so it would not move or fall out.

The Friar
Chapter Four

While the coach traveled over the muddy road, the two Legates were laughing and carrying on and didn't notice they had lost their stolen treasure.

Spilling their drinks and telling each other how brave they were and what King Louis would give them for their merits, they spoke loud and carelessly as the coach passed by the men working in the road outside of Orvieto.

Hector was looking out the coach window, seeing the men, raised his goblet, with his arm stretched out, and shouted something in Spanish. But the men didn't understand what it was and continued to work.

However, Guerino saw something bounce onto the road from the coach but ignored it.

Angelo repeated, "We are brilliant, don't you think?"

Hector replied, "Si, Si, my friend."

No one was the wiser that two of the Pope's trusted Legates had dressed as old Monks and slowly entered the Church of Pope Saint Sylvester the First.

There they sat in different pews during the morning mass. When it was over, and the parishioners left, the two men removed their robes and raced to the altar where they lifted the heavy golden case that housed the skull of St. John and removed the Head, placing it a bag.

As they ran out into the back alley of the Church, they found that it was pouring rain. Looking at one another, they just smirked and attached the bag to the trunk area of the coach.

Then climbing into the coach, they gave the order to the coachman to proceed.

Laughing, the men tried to second guess what the King of France would give them as a reward for such a brazen and successful act.

The coachman rode through the narrow streets of Rome neither fast or slow and finally came to Ponte Cavour, where it crossed the Tiber River and where the Royal Louis ship was tied up.

The two men, Hector, and Angelo got out of the coach and went to the rear where the luggage was customarily placed and found it empty with rope hanging down into the muddy road.

Surprised, Angelo first spoke. "What, where is the Head?"

Hector looking at Angelo, was just as shocked and replied, "How can this be? We tied it almost too tight. Where did we lose it since we never stopped?"

Both men were now stupefied and nervous. Neither could explain to the other what went wrong. Nor could they figure a way to tell this to the Cardinal or the King.

Fear came over the Legates. They might lose their lives over such a terrible oversight. They probably should have placed it inside the carriage with them. How dumb!

Rather than leaving that day on the French ship, they decided to wait and see if they could locate the missing Head.

Returning to Roberto's Inn was the only recourse at the moment, and so they told the coachman to return to Venice and wait in case they needed him again.

The Friar
Chapter Five

The extensive St Peter's Square was just off the Vatican.

On non-participation days, it was breezy as few people walked the grounds. But occasionally, there would be pilgrims who would kneel to pray and give thanks.

Here in the Vatican is where the current Pope and his previous Papal Bishops struggled with the Empires of the World.

One such struggle was called The Investiture Controversy, or Lay investiture controversy.

To add to this debate, the Cardinal clergy usually was controlled by the Royal Houses and separated from the Holy See due to distance. Many times, this influence by the Empires placed an additional strain between the Pope and the Kingdoms of Europe.

Strangely, the French Cardinals outnumbered the Italians. And the German Cardinals were only a few because of the conflict between the Popes and the Holy Roman Emperors.

This constant conflict existed as the most significant clash between secular and religious powers since it also dealt with land and money.

Beginning in the 11th century, there was a dispute between Henry IV, the Holy Roman Emperor, and Pope Gregory VII concerning who appointed the Bishops (investiture).

The ending of such lay investiture would threaten to weaken the influence of any Empire or area. So, there was the desire by the Noblemen within the Empires for Church reform.

Typically, the Bishops would collect money within the village or area of the Church and send this to the Vatican. However, the Noblemen owned the lands that would be passed down through each generation, and who generally acquired more land if the Bishop within his territory died without any heirs.

This caused King and the Vatican alike to grapple since it was the King who would appoint a successor, ensuring that he would have a watchful eye over the Noblemen, the lands, and ultimately the money collected.

By granting a Bishop to those families, it provided guaranteed loyalty to the King.

Often, the King would leave the Bishop spot vacant while collecting the taxes himself that would help fill the Crown coffers. By doing so, it rightfully or wrongly diverted the monies that were due the Church, causing this state of argument.

Every Pope wanted to end this lay investiture because it weakened the Pope's authority inside the various Empires and deflated its private assets for building its own vast properties within the Papal States and throughout the World.

The Church argued that only the Pope could name a Bishop to an area because it eliminated any nepotism and provided better Church care for its parishioners.

Hence, Pope Gregory VII issued the famous "Dictatus Papae," which acknowledged that the Pope alone could and would appoint Bishops.

When Henry rejected the decree, he was excommunicated, but through eventual absolution, the decree was removed after Henry performed public penance.

The Friar
Chapter Six

When Paolo and Aldo placed the Head on one of the two wooden operating tables, there was a bright light that almost blinded the two men. It seemed to have a shiny piece of metal inside the skull that reflected the sun.

Stunned, Aldo said to the doctor's assistant, "This Head or whatever it is scares me beyond belief. I am sure it is haunted and wicked. Perhaps it even houses the devil, so I must take my leave. Sorry, but I must go!"

Paolo understood since he had never seen anything like it in his twenty-eight years, and he'd been a nurse and assistant for nearly nine of those years.

Though not superstitious, Paolo knew that there was something unique or magical about this skull. He had seen it before but couldn't remember where and decided to leave it be until the doctor had returned.

The Friar
Chapter Seven

Life was incredibly hard in the Middle Ages. In Europe, thousands would perish through famine, disease, and relentless wars.

Wealthy households and kingdoms pretended that life was good, but for most people, including Noblemen and farmers alike, the threat of war was constant.

Religion and the local Priest became the glue, holding everyone together during the worst of times.

Sometimes the smallest of chapels overflowed with parishioners before or after a catastrophic event.

Likewise, a Monk's life was unpretentious. So much of the time, Priests and Monks alike paid the high price of death, by either dealing with the sickly or taking up a sword to protect the parish.

Becoming a Monk was available to everyone, no matter what class you came from. However, it was generally only for those who didn't want to go to war or hide away from the disastrous life that existed on the outer side of the monastery walls.

Becoming a Monk was simple enough, but the vow of obedience was the initial test, that paved the way to periods of additional tests to make sure that he was ready for this life.

Sometimes it took years to take the final solemn vow, after much practice and service within and outside the monastery.

From different Saints, many separate orders of Monks developed and sprung forth during those changing times:

1. 1091 – the Cistercians were a branch of Benedictines, located in the Citeaux Abbey, near Dijon.

2. 1664 – the Trappists were a branch of Cistercians, situated in Normandy.

3. 1084 – the Carthusians were an Order of Saint Bruno, derived in the Chartreuse Mountains in the French Alps. They included Nuns and Monks.

4. 1216 – the Dominicans, were founded by the Spanish Priest, Dominic of Caleruega, in Toulouse.

5. 1209 – the Franciscans, were established by St Francis in Umbria.

6. 1243 – the Augustinians were founded by several communities of Tuscan Monks that united as a group to follow the Rule of Saint Augustine.

Niccolo, who was just a Friar and in the incredibly early stages of becoming a Monk, was closest to the Benedictines' side, with the vows of obedience, chastity, and poverty. Yet in his young life, he was unsure if that was the way he wanted to live for the rest of his days. He liked the freedom that he had as a mendicant, visiting the various communities, besides being called upon occasionally by the Cardinals and Pope. So, he didn't want to change this and be isolated in any monastery, even if it meant the guaranteed two meals a day and all the wine he could drink.

As a Friar, Niccolo was a "religious brother" or lay brother, who was not ordained but committed to following Christ. And though he was designated as a Benedictine, he wore the robe of a Franciscan.

Most monasteries grew their fruit, vegetables, and grapes for wine. They also grew hops for the beer they made for themselves and the local community.

During various festivals throughout the year, the local monastery would hold a fest to honor a Saint, which bound together Catholic and Pagan traditions. One symbol that epitomized the two beliefs was the Celtic Cross.

It appeared in Ireland and Britain during the Early Middle Ages as the Gaelic symbol of the Celtic Sun and the Christian Cross.

Some believe that Saint Patrick introduced the Celtic Cross to Ireland when he converted the Kings from paganism to Christianity.

For Monks, the hardest vow to keep was chastity. It was rigorous and intended to prevent monastics from giving in to their urges of lust. However, this did not exclude the Vatican, where lascivious behavior seemed to overflow, along with controversies inside the monastery walls of many clerics breaking this vow.

Daily prayer was recited at least four to eight times each day.

Technically, Monks were not allowed to leave the monastery for any reason. Everything that they needed was available to them inside the walls of the grounds, including education, food, spiritual guidance, and medical care. Should a monastic desire to leave the order, there would be a formal hearing to determine the motive and purpose for dismissal.

In many villages and towns, monasteries for Monks and convents for Nuns lived outside of town in two separate communities.

During the early years of the Renaissance, a Monk, Martin Luther attacked the Catholic Church and the Pope in 1517 when he wrote the "Ninety-Five Theses or Disputation on the Power and Efficacy of Indulgences" and tacked on the church door of All Saints in his hometown of Wittenberg. Thus, it sparked the German Reformation.

Martin's complaint stemmed from the fact that a Dominican Friar came to town to sell indulgences for the rebuilding of St. Peter's Basilica. After protesting this to his own Bishop, it seemed to fall on deaf ears. Thus, Luther displayed his questions and concerns on the Church door.

In particular, throughout Western Europe, the Roman Catholic Church was as powerful as any other country.

The Church guarded its position against friend and foe alike. Many were labeled a heretic and were burnt at the stake if they went against it.

Money played a significant role in both the wealth and power of the Catholic Church.

Directed by the Vatican to the local Bishop and village Priests, the parishioners were told that they had to pay for their salvation. It was just one of the ways that the Church raised revenue.

Other ways the Church raised money:

1. Selling Relics that were sanctioned only by the Vatican.

2. Selling Indulgences, that were documents produced in bulk and pre-signed by the Pope that pardoned a person's sins, giving them access to heaven.

3. Going on a Pilgrimages to some place of worship owned by the Church that required money for entrance and trinkets showing that you made the journey.

The Friar
Chapter Eight

Through a series of secret French Musketeers who rode from Rome to Paris, they delivered the news of the missing Head, to the Captain, Gerard Bouche.

Now galloping up to the gates of the Versailles, the Captain of the guard saw that they were closed. Arguing with the two guards, who did not know who he was, they told him that the King had gone to the "Chateau de Marly." However, Duke Philippe was there, and they were not supposed to let anyone enter or leave without the King's explicit orders.

The Chateau de Marly was at the far end of the grounds of the Versailles, where a little community existed, and the King would take most of his mistresses there to flee from the daily rigors of the court.

Peering down from his horse, the Captain said to the guards, "I will have your heads if you don't let me in!"

Just then, one of the guards saw a flicker of sunlight bouncing off the King's gold "Fleur De Lis" imprinted on the horse's bridle.

He dashed to the center of the gate and apologized profusely as the Captain charged throw the gates.

Riding up the path to the main doors of the Palace, the Captain rode as fast as he could dismounting swiftly as the groomsman took the reins allowing the Captain to run up the stairs to the Duke's chambers. There he burst into the rooms finding Philippe and another, Chevalier de Lorraine, in a passionate embrace.

Excusing himself, Chevalier said, "Captain Bouche, apparently you are more important at this very minute. Otherwise, you would not have interrupted us, I trust?"

The Captain, though not a prude nor unfamiliar with the gossip of the Palace, replied, "Monsieur Chevalier, I beg your pardon, but this is of national importance, else I would have waited my turn!"

Chevalier smiled, snickered, and then kissed Philippe on the cheek and walked past the Captain, patting him on the right shoulder.

Philippe, who seemed to be entertained by this vocal jousting, said to the Captain, "Well, what is it, man?"

Though the Captain did not know how much Philippe knew about the theft or the plans thereof, he opted at that moment to divulge the whole story.

After telling Philippe about the lost Head, the Duke dismissed the Captain and told him that he would deal with the King upon his return.

Standing outside the chambers in one of the long waiting hallways, Guy Benoit was biding his time in the vestibule for the Duke of Orleans, when the Captain had burst through the doors running into the Duke's chambers.

It was almost two hours later when Philippe came out of his room after dismissing the Captain and asked Guy to walk with him to the gardens.

Though Guy had met Philippe before, they rarely spoke together since most meetings were usually with King Louis.

The first thing that Philippe asked was, "Do you know anything about the Head of John the Baptist?"

Guy stopped, then Philippe turned around to look at Guy, who answered, "Strange question to ask Monsieur, but yes, I have heard from the other Legates that the Head has gone missing from the Church of Saint Sylvester."

Philippe then asked, "Why do you think the other Legates would have told you, and what else did they say?"

Guy decided to answer correctly and truthfully said, "I am not sure why they informed me other than making a point at dinner, that it must have been the French King to have done something so farfetched due to his relationship with the Pope."

Philippe was looking down at his boots that were now covered in mud from the several days of rain.

Thinking how to respond, he turned to Guy and replied, "Perhaps I am too unaware of the things that occur at court. I will converse with the King and find out the truth. I am sure we, as a country, do not need anything else exploiting it. In the meantime, what can I do for you?"

Guy, sensing that Philippe was bewildered by this report, told him that the Pope would like to meet with Louis face to face to discuss the Jansenism dilemma.

Philippe, replied, "Sir, I am afraid that will never happen unless the Pope would come to France! But I will inform Louis at our next meeting."

Then Philippe turned and walked towards the doors of the Palace as Guy stood there for a moment, trying to understand the Duke's response and if there was anything else, he could do?

The Friar
Chapter Nine

Europe in the Middle Ages was continually changing as wars, the plague, or other natural disasters divided up territories, cultures, and religions.

In 1378 through 1416, there was The Western Schism, or Papal Schism, when two or more claimants for the See of Rome existed. In other words, two Popes ruled as the true Pope.

However, with strong French influence, starting in 1309, Pope Clement V, decided to move the papacy because of political considerations, to southern France in Avignon, where it stayed for the next sixty-nine years.

Of course, this caused much confusion, and the once importance and effect of Rome declined without its Pontiff.

Though a Frenchman, Pope Gregory, returned the Papacy to Rome in 1378, disharmony continued amongst the Italian and French religious assemblies.

After his death that year, the conclave of Cardinals elected an Italian, Pope Urban VI.

This election caused more hostility within the Cardinals of France. So, they, in turn, elected their own Pope, Clement VII, who returned to Avignon.

Subsequently, for almost forty more years, there were two Papal houses.

Each Pope would lobby the Kings of Europe for their support, all the while playing each of the Crown Heads against one another.

Fed up with the situation in 1409, a council assembled in the town of Pisa to end the stalemate.

They then declared that both Popes to be controversial and went ahead and appointed one more Pope, creating a third Pope when the other two would not give up their tiara or miters.

Finally, in 1414, the Council of Constance resolved the issues, and the three Popes became only one, Pope Martin V.

The Friar
Chapter Ten

On a typical sunny summer afternoon, Niccolo arrived at the Inn where the Diplomatic Papal Legates in Rome stayed.

They lived there in between traveling on their missions and journeys for the Pope and the country they represented. Here, Niccolo found a room and a bath in this easy-going guesthouse.

The Roberto Inn, owned by Roberto Santoro, managed the small set of apartments with the aid of a former French prostitute by the name of Louise de Maison Blanche.

Much later, through his own investigations about Louise, Niccolo found out that she had been sent away from the French Palace to a convent.

From the convent, in the southern French town of Menton, she was traded to an Italian family across the border in the town of Ventimiglia.

Inappropriately, as she grew up, Louise learned to use her body for services that eventually brought her to Rome, where she was introduced to Roberto after his wife passed away.

"A Daughter he never had" was what Roberto thought of Louise and told his friends and residents. No one ever knew of her prior life.

Before her death in 1718, sadly, Niccolo managed to find out that she was one of many illegitimate children of Louis XIV, who never acknowledged her. Nor did she ever know who her mother was, but there was some speculation that she was the daughter of Claude de Vin des Oeillets.

Claude was the Mistress of Louis XIV, who was a member of the Madame de Montespan's entourage. After six years of being his mistress, he dismissed Claude after finding out that she was involved in the "Affair of Poisons." She died shortly after that, leaving the child Louise at a nearby convent.

The Affair of the Poisons was a shocking murder disgrace during the reign of Louis XIV. It involved prominent members within the aristocracy that reached as far up as the King's inner circle. There were charges of poisoning and witchcraft that ultimately caused the execution of 36 people.

Meanwhile, at the Inn, The Legates all shared the guesthouse, in hidden separate rooms and flats.

They also enjoyed the beautiful garden secluded in the back of the Inn, where they could stroll in private and undisturbed.

When the Legates left on anyone of their missions, their residences were swept, cleaned, and dusted almost every day to make sure that when they returned, it was a clean-living space.

Roberto was paid handsomely by the Vatican and likewise by the Legates.

Though no longer a prostitute, Louise also profited much from her added attention to details for the housing guests.

Not wanting to add suspicion or further speculation, Niccolo decided to keep his reason for being in Rome to himself. He told Roberto that he was a traveling theologist, and the Vatican recommended his Inn.

Paying in advance for the month, Roberto seemed not to care about the why and where and immediately stopped asking more questions and welcomed the young lodger.

As Louise showed Niccolo his room, which included his own bath, he was amazed by her rare fair skin and natural beauty.

Having just met her, Niccolo didn't know that she had had a hard life, as she seemed to go about her tasks gracefully and politely.

Drawing the drapery away to open the sunlight into his room, Louise opened the windows, and Niccolo caught a glimpse of just the side of her breast as the sun's setting rays flickered into the room. He felt embarrassed for a moment, even looking at her and her feminine body. It was something he hadn't seen in his twenty-three years of life, but deep inside of his brain, he knew he would never forget that image.

As quickly as he could stop gazing, he turned his attention to the bed and asked her, "Does it squeak?"

Louise smiled softly and said in her French and Italian accent, "Maybe a little, but I don't think enough to keep you awake, sir."

Niccolo almost chuckled when he heard that, but quickly replied to Louise, "Please, you do not have to call me Sir. Just my name will do."

Louise delicately smiled back and said, "Oh yes, Niccolo," then left the room.

The Friar
Chapter Eleven

In the various Catholic religious orders, there are significant differences between Monks, Priests, and Friars, though they can be one and the same.

Before St. Benedict wrote "THE RULE," which included the three essential vows, Monks at that time were not Priests.

Neither Monk nor Friar, Pope Clement XI's original name was Giovanni Francesco Albani. Born in the town of Urbino, it was part of the Papal States, who, in 1626, under Pope Urban VIII, conclusively incorporated the Duchy into the Papal dominions.

It had been a gift by the last Della Rovere Duke, which was to be ruled after that by a Papal Legate. Clement later died on March 19, 1721, in Rome, having been Pope between 1700 and 1721.

Born of noble birth, Giovanni received an education in the classics, theology, and canon law. Eventually, he became governor of the Italian cities of Rieti and Orvieto.

Later, Pope Alexander VIII selected him as a Cardinal Deacon in 1690.

Then Pope Innocent XII ordained him in September 1700 to a Cardinal Priest, which allowed Giovanni to say his first mass in October 1700.

When Clement was elected Pope after November 23, in the same year, it was a time when the Papacy held less and less power politically. It was also a time when the influences of Europe were changing within Spain, and Philip V founded the Bourbon Dynasty.

This was to alienate the Holy Roman Emperor Leopold I since Clement recognized Philip, and Leopold accused the Pope of joining the French side in the never-ending rivalry between the families of the Bourbons and the Habsburgs.

However, Clement wanted to avert war by mediation and to avoid disaster within Italy. Unfortunately, he failed, when Prince Eugene of Savoy later ousted the French troops who occupied the upper part of Italy.

This disaster launched the War of the Spanish Succession that lasted during 1701–1714.

Clement thus was in a continued issue with the French complications of Gallicanism (The French Catholic Church), which was an ecclesiastical doctrine that supported limitations of Papal power, and Jansenism, an unorthodox doctrine.

This doctrine also deemphasized the choice that redemption through Christ's death was open to some but not all.

On Sept. 8, 1713, Clement issued his bull, which some French Bishops did not accept, and he ended up excommunicating four Bishops, which was ineffectual.

Clement was also less wise in his condemnation of the Chinese and Malabar rites in a decree of 1704.

The Friar
Chapter Twelve

Throughout his reign, Louis XIV sought Absolute Monarchy as one great ruler.

He had decided to do away with the Chief Minister position after his friend, educator, and closest ally Cardinal Mazarin died.

Mazarin had been Richelieu's assistant and Louis XIII's Chief Minister.

In the middle of the 1600s, The Fronde, which was the civil war of nobilities fighting the King, took place. Ministers and nobility alike were imprisoned if they disagreed with the King.

One such significant affair occurred before his death in 1673 when the famed Musketeer, D'Artagnan, arrested the former Superintendent of Finances, Nicholas Fouquet, for embezzlement and treason. Fouquet was imprisoned from 1661-1680 and later executed.

Even though there was a King, there existed a limited power clause that was written in 1302, called the "Estates General."

This so-called power was made up of the clergy, nobility, and commoners. It was never used or summoned by either Louis XIII or Louis XIV until years after their deaths.

Louis XIV sought to be Europe's King and used Pope Clement's help from time to time but also argued against him in both religious and civil matters.

One such major issue for Louis was the French Huguenots, otherwise known as the Protestants.

Though granted freedom of religion by the Edict of Nantes in 1598, to protect their rights, Louis XIV revoked this right in 1685 that prompted their mass exodus and violence throughout France.

Louis thought that it was a prudent decision but backfired and had a tremendous impact on the economy and taxes since there were an estimated 800,000 Huguenots in France at that time.

Louis's younger brother, Philippe I, Duke of Orleans, died at the age of sixty, not long after the incident of the stolen Head and arguing with Louis over the situation of the Protestants.

The Duke of Orleans had been a fierce Commander on the battlefield, yet he was thought to have spent more time with his male companions than with his two wives, even though he did have four children.

Louis would die on September 1, 1715, trying to end the French Wars of Religion. It burdened his everyday existence that was propelled by his secret marriage to Madame de Maintenon, who was a devoted converted Catholic, that was raised as a Protestant, even though she was baptized Catholic.

Under the Peace of Augsburg of 1555, it stated that the religion of the realm was that of the ruler. Despite his efforts, Louis had little control over the ever-growing Protestants throughout France.

Trying to turn the tide, Louis continued to persecute and discriminate against the Protestants by disallowing marriages to Catholics and forbade them to hold official office positions.

Using military force, he established an Edict against the Protestants that erupted into massive violence. Pope Innocent XI argued with Louis that this would not help him throughout the European community, but Louis turned his back on the Pope by telling him that it was none of his concerns. Neither Pope, Alexander VIII nor Innocent XIII was able to persuade Louis.

After Philippe's death and his son's terrible death in 1711, Louis became more anxious to stem the tide of the Protestants with Madame Maintenon, convincing him of his Godly status.

He also focused on obtaining a substantial part of Spain.

Nonetheless, he became a man on a mission who didn't accomplish either and died in 1715.

The Friar
Chapter Thirteen

Returning to the Palace of Versailles from the Chateau de Marly, Louis and Philippe's tête-à-tête was more of an argument about the stolen and now lost Head.

Louis said to his brother, "I just had a disagreement with my wife, and now I must have one with my brother over the same issue. How can this be? Why is such a charade, a concern for everyone else?"

Philippe responded, "Louis, you must have known that it would deepen the rivers between the Papal house and ours, not to mention the rest of Europe?"

Louis laughed and said, "This wasn't supposed to have been known to you because of any ramification. Stealing such an item from a sacred place, so near and dear to the Pope, would have certainly brought him to my table and my thinking."

Philippe shocked was shaking his head and replied, "This may have been the craziest idea yet since Spain and the Emperor of the Holy Empire would undoubtedly side with the Pope, which would only delay resolving the war against Spain."

Louis reminded Philippe, "Might you forget that I am King and that you need to mind your own business unless I ask for it!"

Once again, Philippe had to back down from grabbing his brother and shaking the life out of him. It wasn't the first time he felt that way, but unfortunately for Philippe, it was nearly the last time.

The Duke's days were numbered by bad health, and at the age of 60, suffered a stroke in his son's presence.

During the argument, the King told his brother that the Pope would have to concede that France was not to blame, especially since the King is the proprietor of the Church's wealth, and without the protection and involvement of France, the Catholic Church would cease to exist. It was an arrogant position that Philippe could not support.

Over the years and during many Popes, the King of France was a religiously devout person, yet demanded that the religious strife's of France country were no concern of any other country, let alone the Pope.

After his so-called marriage to Madame de Maintenon, both the Pope and Louis agreed on one issue: Jansenism.

It was created in 1638 by Dutch Catholic Bishop and Theologian, Cornelius Jansen, who stated that only some of humanity would be saved.

Ironically, many inside the Palace believed that Maintenon and Louis never married, since no documentation was ever created, yet she carried much power and influence. And she pressed Louis on this matter.

The Pope and Louis never met in person and only communicated through the Legates and secretaries, and the Pope believed that sometimes what was said to each other was not quite the truth. But it was the only way since neither wanted to be in each other's territory.

Nonetheless, both Pope Clement and Louis fought side by side against the Reformation to return to early Christianity thinking.

The Friar
Chapter Fourteen

Italy had prospered immensely during the beginning into the middle of The Renaissance. It had created its importance, despite the many Noble families, wars, and political upheaval of the merchants and bankers.

It was a time of accomplishments and social changes. It was also a time when so many Italian States became a wealthy power through its local trading.

The Papal States that included Rome along with The Vatican were all affected by this Rebirth.

The incredible artistic and architectural brilliance that came with the Church's blessings included artisans Michelangelo, Brunelleschi, Bramante, Raphael, Fra Angelico, Donatello, and Leonardo da Vinci, just to name the most famous craftsmen.

While Nepotism plagued the Papal Offices with wealthy Italian families, the Pontiffs during this period would typically secure positions and palaces for their family members. In this way, it established the Pope as another secular ruler that crusaded to defend and increase his territory.

Every Pope had vast construction plans that contended with other Italian noblemen and lords. Hence, the Papal treasury spent lavishly on both private and public works. One such construction was St. Peter's Basilica, which was built on the old Constantinian basilica site.

Freethinkers during that time included philosophy, poetry, classics, rhetoric, and political science. It also fostered a spirit of humanism which influenced the Church.

Nonetheless, along with this growth in every corner of Europe, came critics and tyrannical repercussions that resulted in deaths of immeasurable amounts.

Pope Clement, despite his efforts, had unknowingly created his own tragedies and misfortunes during his Pontiff.

The Friar
Chapter Fifteen

Joining in that first evening for supper, Niccolo enjoyed Roberto and Louise's company.

They had prepared a splendid meal fit for a king since they had one new guest, and the Italian Legate was returning from his mission to Paris.

The Legate's last name Rossi (which meant redhead), was born in the Italian town of San Remo.

As Rossi told of his life, for Niccolo's benefit, all learned that his father was a leather maker, with fiery red hair and freckles.

Niccolo intrigued by this distinction asked, "Isn't that unique?"

Rossi replied, "Si, Si, unique for an Italian. I was often kidded that I was born somewhere else to other parents and that I was an orphan."

He went on to explain. "My mother came from Bologna and had black hair, and olive skin, while my father was born in Sicily."

Angelo continued. "Yes, history does say that red hair was unique. But the lineage was from the

Celts and the Scandinavians that gave Galileo his trademark of red hair, who was born in Pisa. And let us not forget the very talented composer Antonio Vivaldi, born in Venice, had red curly hair who his friends called "il Prete Rosso'."

The Italian Legate continued his story as Niccolo, and Louise became sleepy.

He said, "I came from an affluent family, and was able to grow up amongst private tutors since my father made a good living making the leather for royalty and commoner alike."

Seeing that Roberto was beginning to become drowsy, Hector asked, "Another glass of wine?"

Roberto snapped out of it and replied, "Si!"

Angelo continued. "When I was sixteen, I was sent to live with my Uncle, the great Cardinal Alessandro Auditore. He was my mother's brother. The Cardinal traveled to France much of the time and took me along, where I was able to learn the French language with ease."

Angelo paused, smiled, and looked at Hector, then at Roberto as Niccolo and Louise with their heads on the table slept.

Hector urging him on, said, "Well, what else, we need to know."

"Well," Angelo replied. "Besides learning the language, I became good at keeping track of money collected from the Bishops throughout France in the various journals that the Cardinal was obliged to follow. Becoming an expert at this task, I then found myself promoted to a Papal position called "nuncio." After that, I was always referred to as "Rossi Nuncio.""

Hector pounded the table and said out loud, "Great story, don't you agree?"

Waking Louise and Niccolo, they almost jumped up out of their chairs from the sound.

"So, lad, what say you?" asked Rossi of Niccolo.

"What brings you here, and where are you from?"

Niccolo deciding to tell them the truth of his upbringing, he left out his association with Pope and his real reason to be there.

"But you can't tell us who the wealthy gentleman is that you are working for?" asked Rossi.

"No," replied the young Friar.

Hector chimed in. "Oh, too bad, we might have been able to find something else that he would find interesting."

Niccolo continued, "Secrecy is always important to not increase the price of an item that my buyer is searching for. Once told who he might be, the seller will try to change the agreed price. So, it's better to be quieter in such matters."

"I see," replied Rossi, and then everyone continued with their supper.

The evening's meal that Roberto prepared was a type of Gnocchi that could have been created and served in Verona. It was his wife's old specialty. Alongside this, there was fish and cabbage, sprinkled with herbs from the Arab countries. Roberto had swapped some other homemade treats with his friends at the farmers market to obtain these rare spices.

Rossi was very chatty about his trip to Paris and the wonders that he found and, of course, about the ladies within the grounds of Versailles.

In watching Louise's reaction to Rossi's stories, Niccolo sensed that she hated what she heard, but said nothing to stop the Legate from carrying on about the Palace.

Hector Del Rio, the Spanish Legate, had joined the small intimate group after the dinner had started and only picked at his meal listening to the boosting from Rossi.

Occasionally Del Rio, being of Italian and Spanish descent, would say a few things in his broken language, "I've been there before and was not impressed by the vulgar shenanigans that went on within Louis's purview."

Hector, Roberto, and Rossi bantered about for hours while Niccolo and Louise listened until their eyes closed again.

Finally waking himself back up, Niccolo excused himself to retire for the evening, but not before he nudged Louise to do the same.

Since the kitchen had been cleaned up by Louise, she was able to go to bed, as Niccolo walked her to her chambers, smiling and saying goodnight.

Climbing into the strange bed for his first night, it proved to be a nightmare of dreams in between his waking up and thinking about Louise's breasts. It seemed not to want to leave his brain, and Niccolo wrestled with her vision all night long.

In the morning, when he went downstairs to grab a roll and some wine, Louise was standing over Roberto's unconscious body in the kitchen.

She didn't know if he was dead or alive, as she turned to look at Niccolo.

"What happened?" the young Friar asked Louise.

"I do not know," replied Louise. "I came back in from throwing away the garbage, and he was like this? Is he dead?"

Niccolo stooped down and touched the back of his neck and said, "He is still alive, but we must fetch the doctor. Please and hurry!"

Louise ran as fast as she could pass the marketplace to where the doctor lived and proceeded to tell him what had happened.

Grabbing his bag, the doctor and Louise then ran back to the Inn, just as Niccolo turned Roberto over and was trying to pour water down his throat.

The doctor yelled, "Stop!" then thanked Niccolo and told him that he would take over.

The Friar then took Louise's hand and walked her outside to wait for the doctor's findings.

About an hour later, the doctor came out to discuss Roberto's condition.

"Apparently, he has had a heart attack," the doctor announced.

"He must have bed rest for a couple of weeks so that he may recover."

Louise was stunned. "What should I do?"

The doctor said, "Louise, you and hopefully Niccolo can lend a hand while he is bedridden? Roberto told me to ask you, looking straight at Louise, if you wouldn't mind managing the property until he was well enough to get around."

Louise replied, "Well, yes, but only if I can employ Niccolo?"

Niccolo was dumbfounded but agreed if he could between his travels. He did have more important tasks on his mind, "the missing Head!"

It was clear that no one at the time, including Niccolo, understand the real reason for Roberto's heart attack.

Poison had been the culprit that had been slipped into Roberto's wine without anyone knowing.

61

Evidently, after Niccolo and Louise retired for the evening, one of the Legates emptied a tiny amount from a vile into Roberto's goblet as they were all laughing boisterously and then the three men toasted for a bright future.

Since it was just a test, Roberto slid to the floor unconsciously moments later.

The Legates quietly laughed, acknowledging their efforts, and smiled at one another. They now knew that they could plan their attack on the Pope, as requested by Cardinal De Noailles.

The Friar
Chapter Sixteen

Missing from the Inn during this episode with Roberto was the French Legate that no one seemed to take as a serious problem.

According to Rossi, Guy Benoit was very rarely there and usually in Paris or Versailles, or visiting The Pope, but Niccolo thought it strange, considering Roberto's heart attack.

As the weeks went by, the Friar reported back to the Pope what he was able to find out.

Niccolo said, "Even though I haven't been able to locate the Head, I feel that I am getting closer each day."

Then asking the Pope about Guy, Clement dismissed Niccolo's question. He seemed to be preoccupied with the Head of St John, so Niccolo didn't bring it back up again.

The other two Legates came and went every few days or so, and Roberto slowly regained his health with Louise proving to be an excellent manager and nurse.

The Inn where the Legates resided was on the street called Via Liguria. It faced the Medici Villa, and from there would take Niccolo about forty minutes to walk to visit the Pope unless he took a carriage, which only took fifteen minutes.

When Niccolo walked, he would have to cross the rickety bridge at the Ponte Cavour.

He'd also pass by the Fountain that the Pope had built for the porters.

These were the men who unloaded the wood, wine, and other commodities from the boats.

It was a pleasant spot to rest, have some water before heading into the craziness of the Eternal City.

Rome was also known as Caput Mundi (Capital of the World), as noted in 61 CE by the poet Marco Anneo Lucano.

Then Septimius Severus (145–211 CE), the Roman Emperor called Rome, "The Urbs Sacra" (The Sacred City). It was not based on Christian Religion but rather as the sacred city of the Roman religion.

As the weeks went by, sometimes Louise would follow Niccolo along to the Fountain and then return to the Inn, never crossing over the bridge into Rome. Niccolo always thought this was odd, but never pressed for her reason.

Once after they had passed through their neighborhood, Louise stopped walking and took Niccolo's hand and placed it on her cheek, and said to him, "I think I am falling in love with you."

Niccolo, with a big smile, said, "And I with you. I believe that God has placed the two of us together at this very moment, and it thrills me to my core."

Walking by himself on this particular warm sunny day, Niccolo arrived at the Fountain to see both Rossi and Hector stepping onto a French ship in the small harbor.

Tied to the dock, in the Tiber (Tevere), the Royal Louis was pointed towards the Mediterranean and looked like it was just about ready to sail away.

Niccolo thought it odd that two of the Vatican Legates would be on the same ship, particularly since the two countries were at war at that very moment.

The Friar
Chapter Seventeen

St. John's Head had a very distinct journey from the time John The Baptist was decapitated.

According to The Holy Scriptures, and because she feared him, John was beheaded by the wishes of Herodias. She forbade it to be buried next to the rest of his body.

John had seen the marriage of Herodias to Herod Antipas as adultery, so Herodias wanted his Head delivered to her on a silver platter.

Through the decades, part of John's Head found its way to the Prodromos Monastery in Petra, while another found its way to the Forerunner Monastery of the Studion, in Constantinople.

Then in 1204, John's Head was seized by the Catholic Crusader, Wallon de Sarton from French Picardy, who then took it to Amiens in Northern France and donated it to the local Bishop, where they constructed a Cathedral.

The relic had been on a silver plate that Wallon had to sell to pay for his return voyage. Some believe it was the original platter given to Herodias.

When a particular light would shine on the skull, it could give off illumination of such magnitude that would cause the nearest persons to gasp.

The Head with crystal-like transparency seems to have been broken apart and ended up in four different locations:

Amiens France of course, with one piece at the Athonite Monastery Dionysiou, in Greece. Another piece was located at the Ugro-Wallachian Monastery of Kalua, Constantinople, or Romania (there are conflicting reports). And the final piece was at the Church of Pope Sylvester's in Rome (Basilica of Saint Sylvester the First, or in Italian, "San Silvestro in Capite" or Latin, "Sancti Silvestri in Capit."

The town of Amiens eventually became the pilgrimage spot for everyone, including the Crusaders, Kings, peasants, and princes.

Then in 1604, Pope Clement VIII requested another piece from Amiens to add to the Head in Rome at the Basilica of Saint Sylvester the First. This marked the most sacred of all the locations for the devoted.

The Friar
Chapter Eighteen

King Louis of France in 1701 had more irons in the fireplace than he should have.

Egos aside, the other rulers within Europe played against Louis as the Americas, and Canada came alive from exploration.

This along with the new sons and daughters within the realms of Europe who became new kings and queens jockeyed for superiority, upstaged Louis's plans. At sixty-one, the old King of France had possibly outlived his own dream.

With the question of what religion would be part of any country, Louis wanted England to return to Catholicism. However, King William pleaded with his countrymen to stay the course and abide by the wishes of the other Protestant countries.

Hence, Niccolo thought, "I may be stepping into a much greater problem than just a missing Head, albeit a famous one."

Walking through a summer storm of wind and rain as it ripped across the bridge to the Vatican, Niccolo watched the French ship sail out down the river towards the Atlantic harbor.

Niccolo finally arrived at the Vatican steps, as one of the Swiss guards nodded to the young man clad in the dirty robe.

Making his way to the top landing, the Friar was out of breath, knocking on the Papal door.

Just then, the secretary opened the door as the winds almost shoved Niccolo inside the chamber.

The Pope smiled at the young Friar as he stepped in front and stooped to kiss the Papal ring.

"Papa Papal, good afternoon. Thank you for seeing me, Your Holiness."

"Niccolo, my son, what news do you bring me on this terrible day?" the Pope responded.

"I am afraid not much, Papa, but I do have questions of concern that you might be able to answer?" the Friar said.

Niccolo went on to tell the Pope of Roberto's incident and the about the two Legates.

The Pope seemed to be perplexed.

"Niccolo, what did the doctor say about Roberto besides being a heart attack? It sounds somewhat suspicious to me that this would just happen!"

"Yes, Holy Father, I've not ruled out perhaps some other factor for his condition, since only the two Legates were with him that night.

Niccolo continued, "More importantly, why would two of your Legates be traveling on a French ship and to where?

The Pope responded. "Might they be connected somehow? I know of their friendship but traveling together would be cause for suspicion!"

The Pontiff continued, "According to Guy Benoit, the latest from Louis was that he wanted my help to squash the riots that his country was having between the Protestants and the Catholics."

Niccolo replied, "To me, as the outsider, Louis is playing both ends of the candle."

"You may be right, my son. I've tried to convince Louis to reverse his stance on the persecution of the Protestants since both sides of Christianity will have to live in harmony, I imagine," replied Clement.

The Pope then said, "Despite Louis' past of being promiscuous, he has taken the high road. I am sure this has to do with Madame Maintenon.

Becoming a religious zealot, due to her influence, he now feels that he must maintain a Catholic hold over his own country. Unfortunately, England, Germany and the rest of Europe are adjusting to their new way of life, outside of Rome."

Clement being a realist, then stated, "The problem is much deeper with the New World of the Americas and Canada also siding up as either Catholic or Protestant."

Niccolo was troubled that the Pope had seen Guy since he hadn't come to the Inn, according to Louise.

"Your Holiness," the Friar started to say.

The Pope looked at Niccolo and responded, "Son, I know you want to know why I have spoken to Guy? Well, honestly, amongst the three Legates, he is the only one I trust with my life! And he is a Musketeer."

Niccolo was shocked for a moment, because it didn't make any sense since he was French, and Rossi was Italian.

Smiling, the Pope said, "Guy Benoit was born out of wedlock by my sister, Serena Albani, to the

French nobleman Luc Benoit from the Loire Valley."

Continuing Clement said, "Though my sister died immediately after giving birth to Guy, his father Luc, raised Guy and presented him to court as his only son, even though he was married at the time to Madame Melanie from Marseilles."

Taking a breath, The Pope continued. "Melanie was wealthy and much older than Luc and had been previously married to a merchant of oil before she passed away, two years after Serena."

Then the Pope said, "Originally, Guy became a trusted groomsman for the King since Luc managed the Royal stables. But as time went on, the King relied on Guy for many other tasks and eventually gave him the responsibility of communicating with the Papacy."

The Pope, who was beginning to sound hoarse, stopped for a moment and took a sip of wine.

"Guy had met Charles de Batz de Castelmore's (D'Artagnan) son, Louis the Elder in 1671, before D'Artagnan, the Captain of the Musketeers died at the battle of Maastricht, during the Franco-Dutch War. The two boys became fast friends, and I am sure that this relationship had a lot to do with

Louis's admiration for Guy, adding him as his personal swordsmen."

Clement then remarked, "It's apparent that Guy is the one person that both Louis and I trust, even when it appears to the other Countries and Kingdoms that we are battling each other. Guy is, after all, a Musketeer that is always called upon."

Niccolo was pleased to find out that he could cross Guy off his list and wanted to meet this man that the Pope held so high.

With the news of Hector and Rossi sailing off in the French ship, Clement told Niccolo, "I will inform Guy and see how it plays out in France."

Clement then said to Niccolo, "Look deep at these two Legates and let me know what you find out. It is a major concern that two of my own confidants may have something else going on."

As Niccolo was about to depart, a knock at the Papal chambers startled them, and the secretary opened the door to find Guy soaking wet from the storm outside.

"Pardon me, your Holiness, I have heard some news that might be of some interest to you!" Guy said.

"Guy," the Pope replied, "We were just speaking of you. Let me introduce you to my other trusted adviser, Niccolo Vitelli."

The Pope continued, "Both of you gentlemen should know one another since I am sure that you will cross paths very soon."

After the pleasant greetings, Guy began to tell his story.

He'd been at the Il Treppio to have a meal when Dr. Perna, the doctor from the town of Orvieto, came in and sat down at the next table.

Acknowledging each other, they soon struck up a conversation, and the doctor told Guy of what had taken place in the town.

Guy informed the Pontiff and the Friar that the doctor had come to Rome to ask the hospital if they could explain why the three men had died apparently after holding a skull.

Guy also said that the doctor went to see his friend, Bishop Corradini, to ask his advice in case of anything religious or spiritual.

The Pope said, "I know Corradini. I ordained him just last year and will be able to request his presence to see what the doctor may have told him.

Niccolo said, "I think a trip to Orvieto might be in order to investigate this. However, should we stay and wait for the conversation with the Bishop?"

"Yes," replied the Pope.

The Pope then asked his secretary to have Giancarlo, the altar boy, fetch Corradini while Niccolo waited.

Then the Friar and Guy spoke about the Legates and sailing on the French ship. This was more of a reason now, for Guy to race back to Paris.

Guy, still dripping from the rain, excused himself to leave.

He then said to the Pope, "I will return to Versailles and find out what the other two Legates were up to and report back as quickly as I can."

As he exited, Guy pushed against the heaviness of the door.

After opening it into the wind and pouring rain, he disappeared.

The Friar
Chapter Nineteen

After Corradini related the doctor's story to the Pope, Niccolo was instructed to go to Orvieto and retrieve the Head. They would have to figure out how it was stolen and by whom in another way.

Niccolo thought that the two Legates might have had a hand in the criminal act, but he would have to wait on what Guy might uncover in France.

The storm in Rome lasted two days which delayed Niccolo from leaving, which was just as well since he needed time to prepare for the long journey.

The Pope outlined for the Bishop what would be needed for the young Friar. He said, "Corradini, do not hold the Friar back from completing his tasks. He is very competent, and I trust his judgment on these matters."

Corradini replied. "Holy Father, I will do as I am told. I shall not interfere but will accompany Niccolo so that our intrusion into the community looks innocent enough. We will return with St. John's Head."

The Pope smiled and said, "Excellent. God Be with You," and blessed the two clerics as they departed.

Returning to the Inn, Niccolo was excited and began preparations for his trip to the Umbrian countryside.

That night, across the river, a spark at a nearby warehouse created a flame that grew as large as a cloud storm.

The guards that protected the Papal apartment were frightened by what they saw and sounded the alarm. In doing so, the Pope was wakened along with the remaining staff at the Vatican.

Stepping outside, they could see the flames rising high as the firemen from the Holy City dashed to the general area of the fire.

Drifting through their window at the Inn, the dusty air woke up Niccolo.

Jumping up out of his bed, he woke Louise.

They had become one during the night, and the young Friar knew he would have to make a hard decision shortly on the direction of his life, but for the moment, he wanted to know what had happened outside.

Running down the staircase, he was out into the street in a flash, naked from the waist up.

Louise had joined him as quickly as she could, dressed in her sleeping gown.

Far from where they stood, the fire had consumed the building where stores of French and Spanish provisions were kept, near the Ponte Sant Angelo, along the river, close to the prison.

A few minutes later, Roberto came hobbling outside, trying to see the fire across town.

Fortunately, Roberto had recovered and was up and about. But he was required to maintain a cautious daily routine, as Louise did most of everything, except for what Niccolo could help her with.

From down the street came a brigade and fire cart that ran past the three dumbfounded people.

As they stood there gazing at the flume of smoke, they all wondered where it was exactly.

By the time it was all over, the buildings had been gutted. Only some of the four sides were still standing.

Before the fire, and during the late afternoon, on the day before he was to leave, Niccolo was washing in the bath when Louise entered the room, not realizing that he was in the tub.

She had been singing to herself and backed her way into his room to clean it when suddenly, she turned around and startled Niccolo, who stood straight up.

For a most prolonged moment, they just stared at each other. And as the sweat dripped from Louise's forehead, Niccolo reached his arms out, and she undid her drawstrings and let her garments fall to the floor before stepping in the water with Niccolo.

Now standing outside, Roberto commented, "There will be hell to pay for that, I am sure. Some of those goods go to the Vatican."

Niccolo replied, "I am sure the governments will replenish them quickly to stay on the Pope's good side. Well, goodnight again."

Then Niccolo and Louise walked past Roberto as he continued to strain his view in the direction of the fire.

As the starry-eyed lovers climbed back in their bed, the proprietor was none the wiser as they drifted off into a lover's sleep.

Except for the fire interruption, Louise remained with Niccolo till he was dressed in the morning, for his journey.

At daybreak, the air lay heavy throughout the streets. All the people of the Eternal city chatted about the fire and who or what could have caused it.

No one knew except for Hector and his pal Angelo.

Because they had lost the Head, the Legates decided to cause a diversion to offset any suspicion on them regarding the skull.

At breakfast, both Legates appeared without mentioning the fire, which seemed strange to the Friar.

Niccolo said to Hector, "Didn't you hear the fire alarms last night?"

Hector replied, "No, Senior. I had my ears plugged up, and I slept like a baby. Nothing disturbs me."

Angelo then asked, "What fire?"

Roberto, who was listening from the kitchen, responded, "Really, you didn't hear or know about the fire across the bridge. It was awfully close to the Vatican?"

"Nope," replied Angelo. Then said, "I may have been in my tub, and sometimes I can't hear too good anyway."

In his mind, Niccolo thought otherwise. He knew they had something to do with it, but it wasn't his place to find out and would leave it to be for the polizia.

After breakfast, Niccolo told Roberto he'd be gone for several days.

Angelo asked, "Where you headed?"

The Friar replied as he looked Angelo directly in his eyes, "I'm off to Orvieto. I need to investigate some findings from the local priest. Apparently, he found something of value and wishes for me to see for myself."

Louise acted surprised but already knew of Niccolo's intentions.

Angelo, who was trying to find out more, said, "Well, I hope it has at least some value for you to travel that far?"

Niccolo responded, "I am sure it will. I am traveling with a Bishop who knows the community. Maybe you know of him, Corradini?"

Hector spoke up, "Yes, I do. He's the Bishop that the Pope calls on from time to time."

"Yep," replied Niccolo.

The Bishop, who was leading the trip to the rural town, was late. Niccolo would find out that this was his usual personality. He was even late when he was called to the Vatican.

Being late, was one of those things that the Friar detested from the clerics. They would act like spoiled children and demand respect for their position but would only give it back if they were belittled.

Though the trip would take almost eight hours to travel the sixty-plus miles by cart, the Bishop and the Friar became close friends in telling stories of their lives and the Pope.

Niccolo all the while couldn't keep Louise out of his mind. And in the moments of silence in their travel, Niccolo thought he could be in love with Louise.

But over and over, he'd asked himself, "Is this what I fell, Love, since I have never felt it before?"

He wanted to ask Corradini but decided that it was too soon and that it probably was not the right thing to ask a Bishop. But then who would he ask?

Thinking on it more, he decided that the next time he could, he would kneel in a Church and seek the answer. For now, he had to try and keep his mind on recovering St. John's Head.

The Friar
Chapter Twenty

In the quaint hamlet of Marly, about seven kilometers northwest of Versailles was the Chateau and estate of King Louis XIV.

Alexandre Bontemps, Louis's valet, and Governor of Versailles was ensuring that the Guards that protected the King were ready to return to Versailles, along with the King and his guests.

Except for a small cadre that always stayed behind to protect this small village, Bontemps was the most trusted of all members of the King's inner circle outside of his brother, Philippe.

In the year to follow, both his brother Philippe and Bontemps would pass away, leaving Louis friendless, and only having to trust his so-called wife, Madame de Maintenon.

Before Maintenon, countless courtesans frequented Louis's chambers at Marly. Amongst the more famous was Mademoiselle de Grancey, Duchesse de Roquelaure, and Julie de Guenami.

On this day, however, Louis seemed a bit anxious and annoyed by Maintenon and expressed to her his dissatisfaction in Bontemps's presence:

"Madame, please try and remember that I am the King, not you. Should you wish to try and overtake my importance, you will surely see yourself located far away from my attention."

Bontemps was not surprised since he had heard this before, but he was amazed that Louis would place Maintenon on the same level as he had done to other court ministers and courtesans.

The King's Valet had been involved with a prior incident surrounding Maintenon.

Because of a lie, the King had required Madame to be gone from his sight and Versailles. She did so on her own recognizance, but later the King relented and sent for her to return to court.

Hence when they got ready to leave, Bontemps was instructed by the King to have Maintenon remain at Marly and only return to Versailles later in the day.

Extraordinary for the King, he asked Bontemps to share the carriage with him as they returned to the Palace.

After assisting the King into the purple covered interior coach, the King spoke to Bontemps.

"Alexandre," the King started the conversation.

Bontemps would rarely hear the King use his first name when speaking to the trusted valet.

"Alexander, has your wife or mistress ever told you what you must do concerning anything important?"

"No, Your Majesty, never! They wouldn't dare!"

"Well," the King continued. "Just this morning, Madame Maintenon, expressed to me how I should continue on this farce with the Pope and the Head of St John."

"What?" Bontemps responded.

Louis looked at Alexandre and replied, "Yes, and she thought nothing of it, which upset me. The King of France taking orders from a woman, even if she is my wife. How dare her!"

Bontemps not wanting to further inflame the King, just shook his head in disbelief and grunted to let the King know that he disapproved of such a careless act by Maintenon.

Nothing more was said about it, as Louis turned his attention to the cutting and landscaping that the gardeners were doing from Marly to Versailles.

Though Bontemps had known about the thievery of the sacred Head of St John, he did not intervene or discuss his opposition with the King.

This was a matter of religion and the way the King saw his role, along with the ongoing argument with the Pope.

Though a fervent yet compromised devotee in the Catholic Church, Louis felt that he alone should have the authority over the Church within France, including the church appointments. This constant clash played out time and time again over his entire life, with the Vatican.

The Friar
Chapter Twenty-One

In 1700, as the World was expanding in new lands, Paris had reached its peak as being Europe's largest city with more than 500,000 people.

From early times, the river Seine had become the primary transportation mode in and out to the Atlantic, Europe, Asia, and the new lands of Canada and the New World.

However, the Seine was also the garbage dump, the bathing facility for some, and the water from which people drank their cloudy fill each day.

Luckily, wine was drunk at each meal to heal and counteract those with sour stomachs and the like.

Besides the barges carrying essential import and export goods up and down the river, the people would swim naked and see the solid waste float by. Sometimes a body would pass their way as they enjoyed themselves in the warmth of the summer days.

The Seine was also pumped into some of the fountains where the public would fill their buckets and carry them up the stairs of the apartment buildings.

There were other types of barges called bathing establishments that would charge a fee where men and women could bathe in separate boats. However, the water still came from the Seine.

Nevertheless, there were some sort of chemicals poured into the water occasionally to help disinfect it. Even so, the people using these barges did not escape from the dirtiness of the river.

Throughout Paris, from the time of his father, Louis XIII, many bridges were built under Cardinal Richelieu's construction plan and the rebuilding of the city. He also undertook to create a new chapel at the Sorbonne, the first college that housed volumes of liberal arts, medicine, canon law, and, in particular, theology.

The first college was created by Robert de Sorbon, in 1253, but established its foundation in 1257, by King Saint Louis.

De Sorbon, was the Chaplain and Confessor for the King at that time. Still, Richelieu was able to construct a new dome on the old chapel, having been inspired by Saint Peter's Basilica in Rome.

Richelieu also built his own extravagant home in the center of Paris that he called Palais-Cardinal.

After his death however, it was willed to the King and renamed Palais-Royal.

Richelieu controlled most essential matters, including military campaigns and religious issues of Protestant and Catholics.

In 1630, the Cardinal required Marie de' Medici, Louis's mother leave the court for the second and final time where she was exiled until she died in 1642.

Following the deaths of Richelieu, in 1642 and Louis XIII, in 1643, turmoil ran rampant across France under Cardinal Mazarin, as Louis XIV was only five years of age.

It was a time when the Cardinal fought with the Nobles in controlling the lands, taxes and the country.

Anne of Austria, Louis's regent mother, and Mazarin taxed the Parisians to the point that the prominent Noblemen of France proposed reforms to change the abuses by the State.

After imprisonment and riots, there became the Fronde, which was the bitter battle between Mazarin and the French Parlement.

Twice during this period, the young Louis XIV and his mother Anne of Austria had to flee the city to escape with their lives.

Because of this, Louis never again trusted the Parisians for fear that they would take up arms against him.

This was a significant reason why he and his court moved to Versailles in 1671. Frightened not only by the Parisians but also by the nobility.

Therefore, Louis moved all influential families, to be his complete control.

By doing this, the Nobles no longer lived on their estates, which allowed Louis to consolidate the power of the State into his hands as the King.

During his entire lifetime, Louis only visited Paris about twenty times.

The Friar
Chapter Twenty-Two

Throughout Paris, and in particular, the Versailles society was formally structured.

Nobles with papers indicating their lineage shared the top rung. And there were four different groups or degrees: Titled, Royal Chamber, Marshalls, Chevalier.

They were followed by minor Nobles who had been granted their degree due to service to France. They were also known as Noblesse de la Grande Robe. These titles were purchased.

Then there were the officials, including doctors, followed by lawyers and such.

The next largest class was the middle class that could include merchants and successful artisans of a craft.

The bottom of the Parisians was the poor that included domestic help, manual workers, laborers, prostitutes, and others with no means of income.

During the early 1600s, the poor were helped by a French chaplain by the name of Vincent De Paul. He arranged for and established the first hospital, Hotel-Dieu, after approaching the wealthy of Paris to contribute to this charitable location. He also founded the order for young women to help feed the poor, where they carried pots of soup wearing their gray skirts and white cornetts.

During his life, De Paul was able to care for abandoned infants, though many passed away. Even so, he built additional hospitals and homes for these children.

To assure Louis as the King, he wanted order in Paris and created a Police Lieutenant General.

Amongst other things, the Lieutenant General controlled street cleaning, food supply, and distribution, and regulating corporations.

With the help of his minister, Jean-Baptiste Colbert, France produced silk stockings, furniture, and tapestries.

Religious orders of all sizes and shapes took hold in France, but primarily in Paris throughout the 1600s, causing alarm, since they were directed by Rome and out of control of the Archbishop of Paris.

Jesuits, Dominicans, Capuchins, had brought along many convents and sixty religious orders that sometimes confused the parishioners since some of the teachings conflicted with another. The Dutch Theologian by the name of Cornelius Jansen was one such whose variation on original sin and predestination went against the Jesuits.

Many followers of this movement were imprisoned by Louis, who did not agree with the Papal doctrines.

Cardinal Noailles was one who played both sides in this ever-changing drama. Sometimes siding with the Pope while appeasing Louis. He would tell the Pontiff and the King whatever they wanted to hear.

As part of his position in the summer, the Fire of Saint-Jean takes place when the Abbe of the monastery of Sainte-Genevieve and the Cardinal as the Archbishop of Paris would preside over a procession and the festivities that include over 150 Monks and Nuns. Though he hated to perform in this role, Genevieve was after all the Patron Saint of Paris.

On this actual night, Cardinal De Noailles, along with Hector and Angelo, stood in front of the crowd as the King in his carriage drove by to participate in the event.

They were discussing the death of Pope Clement —
the when, the where, the how.

Sarcastically, the Cardinal said quietly, "Suppose
someone kills Louis before I become Pope?"

The two Legates looking surprised, then at each
other, started laughing out loud. But the
deafening noise from the crowd masked over
their laughter.

Unbeknownst to them was a half-crazed prisoner
from the Bastille who had just been let out after
serving thirteen years for stealing a loaf of bread
during one of France's worse winters.

The man never saw his family again. Outraged by
his imprisonment, he ran to the carriage to attack
the King.

Hector, standing closest to the carriage, leaped
towards the man with an uncharacteristic motion
by grabbing the ex-convict with the knife before
the King noticed what had happened.

Even the Musketeers were amazed at how fast
Hector had reacted.

Without the Royal Party knowing about the
incident, two guards took the man and placed him
in shackles and disappeared into the dispersing

crowd. The man was never heard from or about again.

When it was all done, the Cardinal, who was still startled, said to Hector, "The King will never know how close he came to his own death. Even so, my Spanish knight in shining armor, you will be granted a reward for such a noble act."

Hector smiled and replied, "Oh, I did it for my Queen, if nothing else. Besides, should she or the King hear about it, it will just add to my credibility."

The Cardinal bowed to Hector, "Well done, my son!"

The Friar
Chapter Twenty-Three

When Bishop Corradini and Niccolo arrived in Orvieto, it was just past dusk and too late to search for the Head or find Father Nardella.

Instead, they found the town's inn to settle down for the night.

Hunger and tired, the disguised clerics decided to eat something first and sat down at one of the large wooden tables, facing the rest of the room.

On the other end of the table sat three men loudly discussing the Head in the road.

The men did not know that the two visitors were religious and proceeded with their conversation.

The Bishop asked the inn keeper's wife to fetch them some food, while they listened to the men.

One of the men said, "I knew it was from France. You could smell the buffons (Italian for clowns), in that coach. Besides what other arrogant bastardo has a blue fleur-de-lis emblem?"

Guerino responded, "But you didn't see it, I did!"

As it turned out, these three men seemed to know that the missing Head had been dropped accidentally from a passing carriage, with the French Royal emblem. But because of where they were when it happened, they didn't do anything about it.

It would appear that the men had been working on the road at the edge of town, where the vineyard connected when the French carriage passed by.

One of the men, Guerino, saw the Head bounce out of the wagon but thought it was just fruit or a vegetable. It wasn't until later when they were done working and walking back that they saw the three farmers: Matteo, Geovanni, and Alessio, who had been picking grapes, runoff.

Curious, the three men approached the spot where the Head rested. Looking down at it, they discussed if they should pick it up. But like the three vineyard workers, they too were superstitious and walked away.

When the meal was over, Niccolo and the Bishop went upstairs and closed the door to their room and began to speak.

Corradini said to the Friar, "I am most troubled by this information of the French. I thought for sure that the Vatican and the French King had made amends and shored up any misgivings over the new religious orders that now exist?"

Niccolo, being cautious in his response, replied, "Your Excellency, there appears to be another issue at hand, that neither of us understands. Maybe the Pontiff knows more, and I will refer to his ability to resolve it. We just need to locate the Head and return it to its rightful place in Rome."

The Bishop agreed, and they extinguished the candle for the night, looking forward to collecting the Head.

The Friar
Chapter Twenty-Four

Louis XIV had compassion for the Parisians during the winter hardships that eclipsed life at the end of the century. However, it was only moments of this empathy before he returned to his arrogant self.

Yet at the beginning of the 1700s was a reality check for the King, who wanted Paris and all of France to be the next Rome.

Times had changed drastically with religion, new territory exploration, and attitudes by not only the Nobles within France but throughout the known world at that time.

Minor revolutions, poor harvests, and new inventions also intertwined themselves into the daily lives of the local people.

The Sun King's light and direction for greatness were beginning to dim, but Louis still wanted to hold on and be supreme.

All the structures put in place by Louis were also beginning to unravel, with wealthy merchants and Nobles assuming more control and local power. The King no longer held complete control.

Within a community, craftsmen and artisans held higher positions than ever before.

All the new religious orders directed by the Vatican were now out of the control of the Archbishop of Paris, whom Louis had placed as the head of religious affairs.

Due to Louis' view on Protestants, and revoking the Edict of Nantes, there was a mass departure from Paris in particular, leaving a void in the taxes that came from these people. Some say there were more than half a million people who left France for other countries, including Canada and America.

The continued maneuvers and concessions that Louis had had to make over the Papacies of Alexander VIII (1689-1691) and Innocent XII (1691-1700) regarding Catholics and Protestants embarrassed the French Catholics.

The King retaliated with the seizure of the Papal state in Avignon and his direct attack on the Papacy. Yet he needed the Pope's help in his support against the Jansenists.

Louis had used the Noblesse de Robe men instead of the Noblesse de Blood to make church appointments. These men then became the

King's personal appointees that he could count on when dealing with the issues of religion. This was part of the ongoing problem with the Pope.

Constant validation of Madame de Maintenon within his own court had become an unwanted disturbance, besides his marriage and her importance in daily decisions.

To make matters worse, a play entitled La Fausse, performed at the Hôtel de Bourgogne theatre by the Comedie Italienne theater troupe, enraged Louis by an unfavorable depiction of his wife. The play was canceled and shut down with the actors expelled from the city.

The Friar
Chapter Twenty-Five

What Niccolo originally thought was that Hector and Angelo had left on the French ship during that stormy day that he had seen them. However, he was wrong since both of them had returned to the Inn. But he knew that they were up to something by not knowing anything about the fire close to the Vatican and by what Guy had told him and the Pontiff.

As it is known, Rome to Paris is around 800 miles as the crow flies.

However, the "Royal Louis," had made its way two days later from Rome to Genoa, some 252 miles where she docked to let off the two Legates traveling to Paris.

Taking this amount of time, Hector and Angelo decided that they could speed up their traveling time to Paris by going on horseback.

They had estimated that they could cover the next 600 miles in less than two weeks, even if they stopped each night to rest. Had they continued with the ship it would have taken them almost a month to reach Paris. They were sure of it since they had traveled that way before.

In Bologna, Guy was just getting up from sleeping ten hours after the grueling horseback ride of the last six days. He knew he was in a race with the other two Legates to reach Paris and speak with Louis. He also knew that they were at least two or three days ahead of him, but he felt that luck might be on his side and that he could arrive in Paris before them since he was traveling alone.

On the third day and sore from being on horseback, the Legates arrived in Torino, taking their time, and barely traveling 30 miles per day.

Meanwhile, Guy had traveled 40 miles each day since leaving Bologna and arrived outside of Milano and camped out for the night rather than going into town just in case the other Legates had traveled his way.

By right, all three men were already tired from just these few days but knew that their mission was to get to Paris as quickly as possible.

As the days passed by, Guy and the Legates were bogged down by rain and mud along their respective routes.

Guy had traveled to Geneva, then Dijon, and finally into the small village of Fontainebleau where a vast forest existed.

The village had housed the royal hunting lodge that included a chapel. With its constant renovations, it later became the Palace of Fontainebleau that was a favorite place to go for Louis XIV when he tired of Versailles.

Oddly and in the meantime, the two Legates who traveled Genoa, Torino, Chambery, Lyon, and finally to Fontainebleau, arriving on the same day as Guy.

In the little hamlet of only 148 people, Guy had found comfort in a couple's home that he had stopped at before in his travels.

They were happy to see him since he always left them with extra food or silver for their efforts to supply him with a bed and a meal.

On the other hand, the fashionable and usually brash Legates stayed at the local inn that often housed no more than another two or three guests on their way to who knows where.

Being this close to the center of France, as the King would have you believe, Guy decided to visit the inn where he might be able to hear some news. Guy was unaware that the Legates were staying there.

He wanted to listen to the latest gossip that frequented Parisians. In this way, he hoped to pick up anything that could be useful in his efforts to support the Pope.

It came to pass that by the time Guy arrived at the inn, the Legates had just left the dining hall and went upstairs to retire for the night.

Hence, the men never knew that all three were at the same location that evening.

Little was revealed in conversation with Guy by the remaining people. So, Guy returned to the couple's home for the night.

In the morning, all three men rode off within a half-hour of each other.

Fontainebleau is located thirty-four miles south-southwest of the center of Paris and about 45 miles to Versailles.

Guy decided that he would take his leisure time to visit with the King and rode to Chilly-Mazarin, where he could bed down for the night at the Castle.

The Castle had been named after the old Cardinal of France and belonged to his Daughter, Isabel Mazarin.

At one time, Isabel had been married to a Noble from the house of Fontenay, in Northern France. He had died in a hunting accident at his castle, and later, it was partially destroyed in the Thirty Years War.

Isabel was an independent woman who the King fancied, but she wouldn't have any of it and stayed away from the court and managed her property that her father had left her.

Riding up to the entrance was a simple road that led to a large wooden and steel door.

There were no guards stationed outside, but once you knocked on the door, two uniformed men stood in your way of entering the Chateau.

From here, you notified the men who you were and what business you had with Madame Mazarin.

As one guard disappeared, the other guard moved into a position to cover the entire door.

Guy, not wanting to appear a dangerous person, stepped back, and waited to be let into the Castle.

About five minutes passed by before hearing laughter and chatter coming from Isabel, telling the guard to let Guy pass.

After hugs and kisses, Isabel took Guy by the hand and led him towards the back of the Castle, leading out past the French doors into the garden area.

Two maids rushed from a side entrance bringing platters of meats, cheese, and fruit. Then a butler appeared with two metal carafes, one with water and one with wine made from the Chateau's vineyard.

Isabel said to Guy, "Please sit down, you handsome man of my life. Where have you been, and what can I owe this opportunity of you showing up on this day?"

Guy was amused but almost blushed as Isabel made a big fuss over his arrival.

He said, "As usual, I am the go-between the Pope and the King and find myself trying to figure out who is being the most truthful."

"Oh," replied Isabel. "Are they at each other's ego or throat once again, he said this or that, but I need your help?"

Guy chuckled.

Isabel knew very well that Louis wanted to be the King of everything, but the fact that his religious convictions held him back allowed the Pope to maintain some sort of power over the King.

As a young girl at Louis' court, Isabel came to realize that the King was like a coin with two sides. One being this ruthless person in charge, administrating the country in peace and war, arguing with the rest of the European Kings. Yet on the other side, wanting to be loving like a father and a lover at the same time.

Fortunately for her father, the Cardinal, protected her against the King's advances.

After her wedding, she was whisked away from the court. It was only then that the continued wishes of her sexually by the King stopped.

Guy then explained the situation to Isabel, leaving nothing out, since he trusted her and she was no longer the King's desire, especially with Madame Maintenon keeping all other female's away.

Isabel was not surprised about the thievery since the King was a control freak.

She reminded Guy, "Remember the years of the hard freeze of the Seine when delivery of grain and other commodities couldn't get from the Atlantic to Paris via the river. Louis went nuts and demanded that the grain be placed on sleds with horses. He argued with the Nobles as he wanted the grain brought to Versailles instead of Paris, while the poor were waiting for their handouts. This caused thousands to perish from starvation. Then on top of that, Parisians found little comfort from the poor harvest that plagued the country for two years in a row. After that, Louis stockpiled what little France could purchase abroad and used the foods mostly for the Versailles court and sent little to Paris to feed on."

That evening after dinner, and all the talk of Louis, the Legates, and life, Guy and Isabel retired together to her bedroom.

Both of them had months of pent up intimate feelings for each other since their last meeting. It was that deep desire of two people that only could be accommodated and fulfilled by lovemaking.

The Friar
Chapter Twenty-Six

Orvieto had been a favorite respite for the Popes with three Papal Palaces built on the rock of tufo (tuff) volcanic stone.

The town, with its population of over 30,000 residents, assisted in the control of the road that stretched from Florence to Rome. Occasionally there was a tariff, that was charged for clearing the rubble off the ancient path of almost 280 kilometers.

With its Papal and cultural influences, the importance of the area concerning Rome became that much more during the Louis XIV era.

The King of France had always wished to rule Italy along with Spain. It was one of his dreams.

Several times the French Royal Army marched into Italy only to exit after negotiations.

The Popes dating from the early 1500s had dealt with the sacking of Rome and would escape to Orvieto. So, the town reinforced the fortress with new walls and an underground tunnel and water system that was called St Patrick's Well. It was created to ensure that the town could withstand a siege for any length of time.

In the morning, crisp air floated over the town as Niccolo donned his robe for the visit.

When the two Prelates left the inn on their way to meet with the local priest, Niccolo felt a little strange as a Friar again.

He thought to himself, "Was it because of Louise or the fact that he hadn't been dressed like this in some time?"

Upon entering the church, Father Nardella turned around as he was placing candles on the offering table.

"Good Morning, Bishop Corradini!" shouted the Priest.

"It is with much surprise and happiness that I see you in our humble church," as he rushed to the Bishop to kiss his ring.

"And Good Morning to you, my friend. It is with much pleasure that I see you once again."

Then the Bishop said, "Let me introduce my young colleague, Friar Vitelli, who works directly for the

Pope on unique circumstances. Therefore, he is with me today to bring back the Head of St John."

"Yes, yes, I totally understand Friar, and it is very nice to meet you!"

Niccolo reached out his arm to shake the hands of the Priest only to be shunned as Nardella turned his attention to the Bishop instead.

Niccolo let the disrespectful moment go knowing that the Priest would very much side with the Bishop since he was his boss and administrator of the parish.

Besides, Niccolo thought, "I have a job to do, and that was the more important than petty grievances."

Irrelevance was not part of Niccolo's makeup, and he quickly forgot about the incident.

After conversing for an hour, the Priest took the two visitors to the doctor's house where the assistant had stored the Head.

When they arrived, there was some confusion going on. The doctor had returned and was scolding the assistant over something.

The Bishop was the first to speak.

"Doctor, we are here to take the Head back to the church in Rome. What seems to be the problem?"

"It seems that my assistant had dropped the Head, which has now caused a crack in the skull," Perna said.

"No, I didn't," cried out the assistant.

He went on, "Aldo and I picked it up from the road as carefully as possible and placed it on the table without incident."

As the doctor and the assistant began to argue again, a gust of wind blew so hard that the Head rolled off the table and fell onto the ground chipping the skull.

In the bright sunlight, as the doctor stooped down to pick it up, a brilliant illumination blinded everyone within its vicinity.

No one moved for what seemed to be several minutes, then the Bishop spoke.

"Gentlemen, God is speaking to us. There is no blame to be had. St John's Head is mystical and magical, and since it is still in one piece, there is no one to blame. We will take our leave now to return the Head to Rome, and its proper place of worship."

But before they left, Niccolo questioned the doctor regarding the cause of death of the farmworkers.

Perna said, "I didn't find anything suspicious with the Head and I believe the farmers had perished from what was familiar to us all called, "field poison," and not anything that was on the Head."

Common to farmers, field poison occurred when farmers inhaled vapors from the rotting vines and grapes after an unharvested season due to too much rain or desert-like dryness. Most of the time, farmers wore bandanas to protect themselves as they worked.

It was then apparent to Niccolo that the farmers hadn't protected themselves and understood the doctor's summation and agreed with his speculation.

Hence, the Friar decided that he need not go any further in his investigation of the cause of death and would now concentrate on who stole the Head and why?

The Friar
Chapter Twenty-Seven

Before returning to Versailles, the two Legates rode to Paris to meet with Cardinal Louis-Antoine De Noailles (born 27 May 1651, died 4 May 1729).

The Cardinal at the time was made the Archbishop of Paris, by Louis. Like Clement, he was only recently, before Pope Innocent's death, created Cardinal in 1700.

Angelo and Hector were there to discuss the results of the poison that they had given Roberto and, unfortunately, the lost Head.

The French Cardinal had been cast aside in the enclave when Clement was chosen to be the next Pope following Innocent's death.

De Noailles still held a grudge and would do anything to obtain the Papacy for himself, even if it meant committing murder.

The Cardinal had gained the trust of the two Vatican connections via the many visits to Versailles. He was able to convince the men that he would become the next Pope should Clement pass away suddenly, since he was the senior French Cardinal of the Vatican.

After listening to the men conveying the calamity of errors in retrieving the Head, the Cardinal said. "Listen, this Head was for the amusement of the King. I am more concerned with the demise of the Pope. So, do not be too worried. I am sure by now someone has found the Head and has returned it to the church in Rome.

The Legates felt relieved that the Cardinal did not chastise them or place them in prison for their lack of success. Hence the Head discussion was over before they could even finish their first glass of wine.

Over dinner, the Cardinal was pleased that the poison worked perfectly on Roberto. So, the three men devised a plan to seal the fate of Clement during their secret mission.

Hector said, "We know that the Pope will not come to France, so we will have to take our chances within the Vatican walls to kill him!"

The Cardinal was surprised by the abruptness of the Spaniard. But he appreciated his feelings since Louis and the Pope continued to ransack Spain of its riches.

However, the King and Vatican were only retaliating for the years the Spanish ruled many of the Italian states and cities, including Milan, Naples, Sicily, and Sardinia.

De Noailles said, "I'd like to think that you and Angelo will be able to dispose of the Pope in a way that it shines on someone else. And that it shall not be linked to any of us?"

Angelo replied, "We do have someone in mind. Actually, it could be one of three!"

"Really," replied the Cardinal.

Angelo smiled and said, "Yes, a young man called Niccolo, along with the tart that works at the Inn, and the innkeeper Roberto himself. He was the one we tested it on, and it worked!"

The Cardinal grinning at the two men said, "Excellent. Then we should figure a way that all three of those people are accused."

De Noailles then devised a plan to have a banquet to commemorate the Feast of the Conception of the Blessed Virgin Mary.

The Cardinal knew that this was Clement's most favorite day and one which the Pope declared a most Holy Day of obligation. The Cardinal also told them that he would attend the honor so that he could see the last breath of Giovanni Francesco Albani, Pope Clement XI.

Sitting upright, the two "Judas Legates" both smiled and laughed and told the Cardinal to leave it to them to make sure the poison was prepared in the wine for the Pope.

Hector then asked, "Your Eminence, would you mind accompanying us to Versailles? I would think that the King might be terribly upset with us over losing the Head. And it might be in our favor if you were there to support us?"

The Cardinal responded in a harsh tone, "I suspect he will be, and my being there probably would not help since he has taken a dislike to me for the moment as I keep asking him about the alleged marriage to Madame Maintenon? But let me think about it and decide, and I will let you know in the morning."

The Friar
Chapter Twenty-Eight

Versailles on a particularly chilly day was bustling as it readied itself for the annual Equinox Ball.

As usual, Louis XIV made sure that his entourage of Nobles had plenty to do during and after the celebrations that were held. The yearly events were a way to ensure he had complete control over his realm.

Philippe, who was still angry with Louis, spent most of his time ignoring and dodging the typical gatherings of the court.

Without a war to oversee for the moment, the Monsieur frequently walked in the gardens, minding his business, and lounged with Chevalier.

But Philippe also spent a great deal of time with his wife, Princess Palatine, otherwise known as in German: Prinzessin Elisabeth Charlotte von der Pfalz; nicknamed "Lieselotte."

When Louis walked into his bedchamber one day, he was astounded that Philippe was lying naked with his wife and eating cherries against her unclothed and glistening body. Despite his desire for the Princess, Louis had longed for such a moment, but cast the thought aside quickly. He needed to stay focus on considering recent developments.

"Excuse me, Brother," Louis stated. "I am here to remind you and the Princess that there is a celebration tonight and that I require your presence at the Ball. I need you to be by my side."

Not making a move, Philippe smiled and said, "Of course, Brother, I wouldn't miss it for the world!"

Louis, smiling, turned, and left while Philippe said to Lieselotte, "He can be such an ass sometimes!"

"And what about Chevalier?" asked Lieselotte.

Philippe looking at the Princess, said, "Oh, he'll be there, but for now, let us create a child of our own. He can't have one!"

That night the Ball was a huge success that included the three Legates in attendance.

Against a massive rectangular table that could feed 300 people, including the King's mistresses, the other two Legates sat close to one another, only separated by Cardinal De Noailles.

Facing the two sides at the head of the table, Louis's First Musketeer, Guy Benoit, was seated between Madame Maintenon and the King's new mistress, Julie de Guenami, Mademoiselle de Chateaubriant.

Julie was also known as Julie de Bourbon, and Julie de Gheneni, and was for all practical reasons, the last mistress of the King. But that had been refuted by many.

Guy found the young girl very informed of the King's business and was stunned by the fact that she knew more about what was going on than probably Louis's own ministers.

Acknowledged by the King, the Legates exchanged no conversations with Louis regarding the Pope during the celebrations. However, Bontemps spoke to each man informing them of their specific times they would meet with the King the following day.

The evening delights of food and wine were plentiful, and the King's favorite composer Lully had traveled from Paris to join in the celebration and present his newest play.

The Cardinal kept his eyes on Louis. During the evening, he wondered if his two comrades could, in fact, poison the King? It was just a thought if he, the Cardinal could benefit from such a move, in his desire to be Pope.

However, the timing was not on their side, and the Cardinal's brief notion was forgotten for the moment, as the evening ended as it had begun without drama.

As sometimes he'd create for the evening, Louis had done so for a new dance, whereby the rest of the court seemed to follow his lead gracefully.

Music was supplied by his old friend, Michel-Richard de Lalande. Though Madame Maintenon did not partake, Julie giggled and laughed her way in and out of the arms of her lover, The Sun King, as they pranced about the room.

Between dances, L'Imposteur by Moliere was performed, but by now, Louis appreciated it more than an earlier version when it was banned.

Jean-Baptiste Poquelin, otherwise known as Moliere, had died one year earlier at the age of 51. However, his traveling troupe performed it in honor of him and the wishes of the King.

De Noailles, that evening, did have a chance to speak briefly with Louis. He said, "Your Majesty, I understand that we have recently frightened the

Pope over an issue. I pray that it was successful and humiliating to the Holy See?"

The King, who had just stopped to rest between dances, was not amused by the comment and replied to the Cardinal, "Mind your manners good friend. We will speak about this tomorrow when I speak with you and your connections."

De Noailles was taken back, as he did not realize that the King knew that Hector and Angelo had been known as his spies.

The Cardinal could only reply, "I understand," and backed away from Louis.

Deciding to leave the celebration, the Cardinal nodded his head towards the two Legates, as Guy made a mental note of the entire incident with Louis and his two Papal counterparts.

Guy, who also watched the King that evening, knew that there was not much he could do, decided to relax into the night's festivities, and danced with Julie, as she had requested.

He'd have to wait till the morning to brief the King.

The Friar
Chapter Twenty-Nine

Arriving back in Rome, Bishop Corradini said to Niccolo, "I don't think you need to follow me to the church, my Son. Not that you wouldn't be welcomed, but I think I need to be the one to place it in its rightful place in Saint Sylvester the First."

The Friar knew what he was saying. The Bishop wanted to take full credit. Niccolo chuckled to himself, knowing that the Pope would bestow his own praise and rewards unto the Friar. It was after all, like most things, political.

The Bishop went on to say, "I wish to say mass for its safe return amongst its local parishioners. And I am sure you have more important things to return to, including reporting this information to the Holy Father."

Niccolo replied, "Thank you, Bishop Corradini. Yes, I must concentrate on who the thief was and why this act was performed."

The Friar then found another carriage to take him to the Vatican.

When Pope Clement heard the news from Niccolo, he fell to his knees and started to pray, causing the Friar to kneel down and follow his mentor.

Afterward, the Pope ordered some tea and sandwiches for himself, his secretary, and Niccolo.

Clement asked Niccolo, "Was the Head still intact after its many travels?"

"Yes, Your Holiness. Perhaps a bit banged up, with a small crack in the skull from falling out of a carriage, as it was later told to us," the Friar explained.

"Whose carriage?" the Pope asked.

"I am sorry to say, but we heard it was the King of France's coach!" replied Niccolo.

In shock, Clement looked up from eating his tuna sandwich and said, "Can this be true? Why would Louis insult me in this manner? I thought we were becoming great friends on the same journey?"

Niccolo could only repeat what they were able to uncover in Orvieto from the workers, which was damning enough.

Then Niccolo said, "Holy Father, the most amazing thing occurred. As the doctor stooped to pick up the Head, sunlight bounced off of St John, causing a bright rainbow of colors. The Bishop blessed himself and told us that God was speaking to us!"

The Pope smiled and replied, "Maybe Friar Vitelli. He does speak to us in many strange forms."

Then silence filled the room, as the Pope tried to think of a response against the King.

Niccolo knew that His Holiness felt betrayed and vulnerable since Louis and he played this game of friend and foe time and time again.

The Pope finding an answer said to Niccolo, "There seems to be always a disagreement over mostly religious issues that, in the end, results in Louis needing something. And it is usually my help against one of the other European countries. We will see what it is this time."

Niccolo could see the dilemma the Pope was in and knew that he needed to step up looking for the thieves and the reason and persons behind the crime.

The Friar
Chapter Thirty

In the morning, Louis was wakened and dressed in the ceremonial etiquette, attended by the Nobles.

Later, he ate breakfast with a few remaining Earls handing him his plates and goblets.

It was a sight to behold in this orchestrated ritual that no other European monarch dared to impose on his or her court.

But Louis was the Sun King. He demanded everything be precisely done, even if the rest of France was just meandering along in their lives.

Following the morning routine, Louis presented himself on his throne to welcome the briefings by the ministers and other appointments.

At precisely eleven-thirty Cardinal De Noailles and two of the Papal Legates appeared and bowed.

The Cardinal was the first to speak.

"Good Morning, your Majesty. We wish to brief you on the shortcomings of our adventures in Italy. And, with the retrieval of the Head of St John."

The King stopped the Cardinal and said. "Yes, yes, I know all about it. Your men lost it in their travels, which I find hilarious but disgraceful. Their job was to obtain it and bring it to France without an incident. Now I must contend with the Pope. This is very unsatisfactory!"

De Noailles started to reply, "How did you know of this calamity, Your Majesty…"

Looking at Guy standing on the side, the King said, "Cardinal, I know most everything that occurs within the Realm more easily than you know. You and your people are not the only spies. There are plenty of persons of the court who wish better pensions and position and are willing to let Bontemps know of it. Which, in turn, is told to me."

Then the King asked the Legates. "Which one of you lost the Head?"

As Angelo started to respond, Hector stuttered, "I am sure it was both our faults, Your Majesty. We had attached it to the baggage area on the coach rather than placing it inside with us. We were a bit concerned about the tales of the Head. Not that we are superstitious, but we didn't want to take a chance."

"So," the King replied, "Now I look like the biggest fool. I am sure that the Pope, my friends, and foe alike throughout Europe know that Louis XIV tried stealing the Head of St John. How could you be that stupid to use my coach?"

The Cardinal started to explain but was again cut short by Louis.

"How thoughtless," the King. "Begone, all three of you. Out of my sight and my court. I must find a way to discourage the Pope of reprisal."

As the three shamed men left the room, they argued with one another over whose fault it was and what they had to do.

It was now apparent to the Cardinal that Guy had been to see the King earlier that morning. De Noailles would have to be more cautious, as he had miscalculated the Musketeers importance.

Benoit was the most trusted agent that the King had besides Bontemps and listened to every word he had to say.

In the morning briefing, Guy also suggested to the King, "It might be a good time to ask for the Pope's forgiveness!"

The Friar
Chapter Thirty-One

Louis knew that he had made a mistake in trying to steal the Head of St John. But it was too late.

The King knew that the only way the Pope would forgive him for such a brazen act of defiance was to ask His Holiness for help.

This time, Louis needed the Pope's help against another religious matter, called Quietism. Its attitude or way of life was a passive withdraw from the world or worldly affairs.

Several mystics within France sought this stillness, as taught by the Eastern religions of Hindu and Buddhism.

The King and Madame Maintenon did not understand either of these religions. They had become fanatics, seeking to preserve the Catholic faith in France by disregarding everything else as heresy.

Quietism had been propelled by the writings of the Spanish priest, Miguel de Molinos. He had influenced Madame Jeanne Guyon, who was considered to be a mystic. And her view of her Christian life was about the union with God.

Raised in convents and by nuns, she felt she had attained an "apostolic state," through her experiences and silence in mediation.

Louis, who needed to appease the Pope, sent him a letter expressing his anger of the efforts of some rebellious French patriots who thought of stealing the Head. Then he pleaded with the Pope to please forgive him for their misgivings.

Completing the message, Louis requested that the Pope intervene in the banning of Madame Guyon and the book "Maximes des Saints."

Finding out that her cousin, Archbishop Fenelon, saw the piety within Guyon, and was part of the Royal Court, the King banned Fenelon.

The Archbishop, who was a tutor, was sent away to the archdiocese of Cambrai for the remainder of his days. He died in 1715.

Initially, Guyon's writings were banned by the Papacy, but later they were retracted. Some of her disciples at the court of Louis XIV included non-other than Madame Maintenon.

The Protestants of Holland, Germany, and many other countries embraced Madame Guyon's writings, which further fueled Louis's dismissal of her articles.

She was imprisoned for years at the Bastille and later released and died in 1717.

After Pope Clement received Louis's letter on Guyon, he threw it in the fireplace and said to his secretary, "Let those that find fault in piety, burn in hell!"

The Friar
Chapter Thirty-Two

Racing back to Rome, Cardinal De Noailles, Angelo and Hector continued to go the plan to kill the Pope.

The Cardinal knew that he needed to do something spectacular in the eyes of the King. He needed this to help promote him to become the Holy Father, moving it back to France once more.

De Noailles' dream of eliminating the Italians hold on the Papacy was in his sights.

The Cardinal knew that Angelo and Hector were his scapegoats and would be eliminated once he controlled the Vatican Seal and the Red Robe.

It was ten days later when the three traitors returned to Rome.

Guy, on the other hand, after discussing with King Louis what needed to be done, rode back as fast as he could and arrived two days earlier.

Time was of the essence in this chess game, as the Pope heard from Guy what had taken place in Versailles and Paris.

His Holiness now understood that the Cardinal and his assassins would be returning to Rome to eliminate him.

Niccolo and Guy agreed that a reasonable distance between the Pope and the three conspirators needed to be maintained. They did not know how or when the men would interfere with the Pope, but they had to be on their guard to protect him.

After returning to Rome, the Cardinal went to his residence at Palazzo Cesi.

The original construction began at the same time as the Basilica of St. Peter, in 1517 by Cardinal Francesco Armellini. Eventually, it was sold to the Umbria Cesi family. Now it belonged to Noailles, but he decided to leave the name in place since it had been the same for over 200 years.

Hector and Angelo returned to Roberto's Inn to eliminate any suspicion of where they had been and what they had done.

Roberto and Louise were pretended to be happy for their safe return, as Hector expanded on their exploits of seeing Versailles and the wonders of it and the court.

Little did they know that by the time they had returned, Niccolo was already back, and waiting for them. He also advised Roberto and Louise of what the two Legates were up to.

Keeping out of sight, the Friar was now cautious as to who these men were. So, he remained behind his bedroom door till supper was prepared.

That evening, as the Legates were dining, Guy appeared, along with Niccolo.

After all the pleasant formalities were extended, Louise, having been tutored by Niccolo, brought up the conversation regarding the Head of St John.

She said, "Have you heard. The Holy Head has been returned to the Church of Saint Sylvester!"

Hector, who was about to swallow some soup, almost choked on it and started coughing so much that Angelo slapped him on the back several times before Hector yelled at him to stop.

Then Hector said, "It was found and then returned? Does anyone know who stole it?"

The two Legates were looking at each other when Roberto spoke. "There wasn't any notification from the Bishop today during Mass that it was even missing, though he was happy for its return. For the parishioners, we were simply happy to see it behind its glass case. Some even went up to kiss the shrine. We heard it had a crack in the skull, but no one noticed, particularly since the light illuminating from the Head as strong as ever."

"Well," Angelo said. "I and, of course, all of us are so happy that through the grace of God, this relic has been found. No telling than who the thief or thieves were. But I am sure they are long gone."

Guy looked at Niccolo and then replied, "Perhaps, but then again, they could be close to Rome or even to the Vatican."

Hector sheepishly said, "True, you never know!"

The Friar
Chapter Thirty-Three

There have been fourteen Popes named Clement.

Except for Clement I, (88-99 AD), who was called Saint Clement of Rome, the other Popes, unfortunately, had vast disappointments in their unsuccessful Papacies.

II (1046-1047) – died of lead sugar.

III (1187-1191) – inherited a depleted College of Cardinals.

IV (1265-1268) – after his death, the Holy See remained empty for three years.

V (1305-13-14) – moved the Papacy to Avignon. After his death, the Holy See remained empty for two years.

VI (1342-1352) – he deemed that all who died of the plague would go to hell.

VII (1523-1534) – (First Medici Pope) – many struggles in succession came from political, military, and religion. He had to deal with the indifference to the Protestant Reformation. This radical reform movement throughout Europe created several denominations that broke away from the Catholic Church, creating many other Christian faiths.

Pope Clement VII was also best known for flip-flopping between alliances, including France, Spain, and Germany. However, he did lean toward the French before his death in 1534 after eating a poisonous mushroom.

Clement VII was inclined to change political views to match those of whoever was the most powerful and wealthy at any given time.

Because of his changing allegiances, Clement VII's detractors, including Charles V, "likened him to a shepherd that had fled his flock, only to return as a wolf."

VIII (1592-1605) – many of the Nobles that disagreed with him were burned at the stake. And he hated the Jews and tightened the laws around them.

IX (1667-1669) – died of a broken heart that the Venetians surrendered to the Turks.

X (1670-1676) – almost 80 when he was elected. He labored to preserve the Kingdoms of Europe despite Louis XIV.

XI – included in this story.

XII (1730-1740) – 78 years old, one of the oldest. The conclave took four months to elect. His Papacy failed at reconstructing the missing Papal States that it had lost.

XIII (1758-1769) – repeated disputes with the Jesuits that came from the progressive Enlightenment philosophes in France.

XIV (1769-1774) – the continued suppression of the Jesuits throughout many of the Catholic countries. Poisoned, yet no irrefutable proof was ever produced.

No other Pope has taken Clement as his name. Perhaps it has to do with so many misfortunes attached to its title.

The current Pope, Clement XI, served 8 December 1700 until 19 March 1721, when he died at age 71.

He was nominated after a combative six-week conclave.

He delayed his acceptance for seven days because of his own self-doubt.

After being elected, he found himself knee-deep in a political quagmire to alter the outcome of the war that ensued due to the succession of the Spanish Throne.

Following Leopold's death, the successor was Emperor Joseph. The Emperor then invaded Italy, obliging the Pope to accept the Hapsburg Archduke Charles as King of Spain.

Likewise, Clement could not avert advances by the Turks in Greece, nor keep control over the Papal territories of Sicily and Sardinia.

He argued with France when he condemned Jansenism. And the French disagreed with the Pope over "Papal encroachment in the internal discipline of French Catholicism."

Later he was in the middle of a dispute between Dominicans and Jesuits in China. This clash was over whether Roman Catholic missionaries in China were right to accept and tolerate ceremonies honoring Confucius.

Though Clement XI did expand the Vatican Library, he seemed to always be at a disagreement with one or more European Kingdoms over the Catholic Church teachings.

The Friar
Chapter Thirty-Four

Louis's marriage to the Queen, Maria Theresa of Spain, was the backdrop for France and Spain to be bound together. However, over twenty-three years, the couple had six children, of which only one would live to be an adult, Louis, Dauphin (known as Le Grand Dauphin).

Yet through Madame de Montespan, seven children were born, of which six survived and were legally accepted by Louis and his court.

Madame de Montespan was the Maîtresse-en-titre. The King's unique and recognized mistress.

There were several others, including Louise Françoise de la Baume le Blanc de la Vallière (1644–1710), Duchesse de la Vallière, and Duchesse de Vaujours. Françoise-Athénaïs de Rochechouart de Mortemart, Marquise de Montespan (1640–1707). Françoise d'Aubigné, Marquise de Maintenon (1635–1719), who later was said to marry the King in 1683 but was never documented. Isabelle de Ludres (1687–1722). Marie Angélique de Scoraille de Roussille (1661–1681), Duchess of Fontanges. And there were others, including a nun in the ever-changing merry-go-round of women in Louis' bed.

During one-afternoon card game at Versailles amongst the Queen and the ladies in waiting, the Queen was losing badly and asked de Montespan a question. "Madame is the life inside you, courtesy of the King or some other tavern rat that you so like to be close to since your own husband is old and nowhere to be found?"

Offended, she was about to answer when the King entered the salon.

Having heard the jealous remark by the Queen, Louis said, "My Dear Madame, perhaps the Queen is having a moment from that woman's time of the month. Besides, it is of no concern of hers since she has failed at her duties!"

The Queen, turning her gaze from the King to the table where she held 'kings,' cleverly responded. "Yes, your Majesty, but not for lack of trying."

The King smiling, took Montespan by the hand to lead her away, and replied, "I agree, but alas, not good enough."

Montespan had been and was Louis's love. However, he lost interest in her after thirteen years and proceeded with numerous affairs.

It seems that it all started after a conversation that she might be instrumental in the King's decision regarding how best to posture France and the rest of the world.

Louis wanted to think that he alone made decisions without brother, lover, or ministers' viewpoints or conclusions.

Ironically, Louis's children with Montespan were cared for by Maintenon, as a governess at the court. Yet, following the breakup with the Maitresse-en-titre, the Marquise de Maintenon became Louis's trusted advisor on religion and reason.

As history looks at both women, they held the same influence over Louis.

Not unlike Montespan, who left court over trust issues with the King, Maintenon also left the court over the same problems with the King.

However, Louis, for whatever reason, sought out Maintenon again and had her return to Versailles, where she remained till his death.

The Friar
Chapter Thirty-Five

Per the wishes of Cardinal De Noailles, there was to be a banquet held at the Pope's Apartment to honor Saint Clement and the Head of St. John.

Amongst the guests, that evening included the Pope, all three Legates, the Priory Priest from the church of St Clemente, Niccolo, De Noailles, and Corradini.

Setting the table was the valet, Pedro De Noailles from Rota, Spain, who was the nephew of De Noailles.

Rota is a small fishing village located in the Province of Cádiz, Andalusia, an essential port for trading with North Africa.

Little did Pedro know that his Uncle was trying to kill the Pope and take over the Vatican.

The Cardinal had arrived early and asked his nephew where the Pope would be seated and what goblet he would use for supper.

After pointing it out, the valet went about his business, preparing other items and decorations for the celebration.

The Cardinal then dropped a small amount of clear poison into the Pope's red wine glass.

De Noailles was almost laughing when Pedro returned and asked, "What's so funny, Uncle?"

The Cardinal responded, "Nothing, my boy, except Life and Death. One minute you have everything you hoped for, and then the next, your dead!"

Pedro didn't understand but replied, "Si, Uncle."

Resting at the Inn, before heading to the Vatican, Niccolo spent time with Louise in his room.

It had been some time since they had been together, and Louise was all smiles and tender during their embrace.

When they had completed their lovemaking, each of starry-eyed lovers bathed the other in the tub that Louise had drawn earlier so it would be warm. As they held one another, they promised their love for all times.

Both Louise and Niccolo knew that they would never part.

The Friar
Chapter Thirty-Six

As the sun was just setting, Guy arrived at the Vatican.

The trusted Legate wanted to ensure that all the preparations had been completed.

Surprised to find Cardinal De Noailles and the other two Legates resting in the waiting room, there was an awkward acknowledgment by each of them, that left Guy concerned.

Going to the kitchen, Guy spoke with the chef and assistants, regarding the food and wine, for the night's festivities.

Walking into the dining hall, Guy found Pedro pouring wine into each glass. Then the valet placed a corresponding napkin over the wine goblet to protect it from the air.

Guy watching the valet asked, "Pedro, is everything ready for tonight? Has anyone asked you to do anything differently?"

The valet looked at Guy and replied. "Well, the Cardinal asked me where the Pope's glass was on the table. He also told me to use the wine from France that he had brought for the celebration."

Guy looked at Pedro closely. Sensing that something was not right, he asked: "Pedro, which cup is the Pope's?"

The valet pointed out the cup, and Guy took it and said, "Pedro bring another clean goblet, and I will bring a different carafe to fill Papa's cup. This one from your Uncle is bad as we had it tested in the kitchen, a short while ago."

Unfazed, Pedro did as he was told since he knew that Guy was the senior Legate and especially close to the Pope.

Inside the Vatican hallway, Guy walked hastily to his office, where his two assistants were busily working at their desks.

Eyeing the chemical table by the window, where it contained vials and cups, Guy set the vessel down and said, "Please check this wine. I need to know if it has poison in it."

One of the assistants walked over and began taking spoonful's of the wine and placing it into two different vials. After adding some water to one of the vials, the other assistant with gloves took the vial and poured it into another cup on the table.

Within just a few short seconds, the wine began to bubble, and the assistant said to Guy, "It's poison, perhaps even boric acid. It would have killed the Pope instantly."

By the time Niccolo arrived, all the other participants for the evening meal were seated in the antechamber, chatting about the recovered Head of St John.

In his office, Guy had been pacing waiting for Niccolo. He had been mulling over a plan on how to arrest the Cardinal and anyone else involved.

Niccolo walking into Guy's office, found him sweating generously as he walked back and forth.

"Niccolo," he shouted. "Am I glad to see you, my friend. We have an urgent issue that only you and I can deal with."

After listening to Guy, Niccolo was stunned. He couldn't believe that someone would want to kill the Pope, let alone a Cardinal.

He said, "Guy, we must play out the hand tonight to see where it leads. We don't know if anyone else is involved, but we need to know for sure. It is a sad story to know that in these times that someone, including De Noailles, would want the Pope dead."

As the evening meal was to begin, the Pope entered the room. Each guest stood in front of their placards, indicating their designated place.

The Pope was the first to speak.

"Good Evening, everyone, let us say grace together as one."

Following the prayer, and after His Holiness had been seated, the Cardinal took his glass of wine and raised it to honor the celebration. As he did, he commented, "To our Pope Clement XI, may he live a long and fruitful life, and for Saint Clement and the celebration of the recovery of St. John's Head. We are also honored to have some delightful wine from my vineyards in France. May it please your palate as much as the food we now undertake."

Just then, Guy, looking directly at the Cardinal, stood up and replied, "Cardinal De Noailles, I hope you do not mind, but we have replaced your wine this evening. For whatever reason, the wine you have brought apparently spoiled on its travels to Rome."

The Pope looked at Guy curiously with an eyebrow raised but said nothing.

The Cardinal surprised and stunned, lowered his arm from holding the glass and said, "What, I am sorry Your Holiness. It must have been set in the sun after fermentation. I will speak with my vintner when I return on my way to Paris.

The Pope smiled and "No bother Cardinal. I believe Guy took care of the issue, and we are now drinking our favorite local wine from Orvieto instead."

As the dinner concluded, an assistant from Guy's office visited the dining hall to whisper in his ear. It had been verified that the wine was poisoned.

Guy never moved or said anything till after his assistant departed.

Looking at the Pope, Guy asked, "May I have a word in private with His Holiness, before you retire?"

The Pope, who knew that Guy could be trusted, excused himself from the dining hall and said goodnight. Then he and Guy exited to the Pope's bedroom.

Meanwhile, the Cardinal looking as if he had become deathly ill, said to the rest of the guests, "I am sorry, but I must take my leave. I am needed back in Paris and must rest for the early morning travel."

The two silent Legates Hector and Angelo bowed to the departing Cleric and then said that they would head back across the bridge to the Inn for the night.

Niccolo continued small talk with the Bishop and the Priory Priest, but only for a few moments then excused himself. As he reached the doorway to the outside, he ran down the stairs to the stables. There a horse had already been saddled for him. Galloping towards the Inn, the young Friar ran the poor horse hard in the late hours of the night.

Inside the Pope's bedroom, Guy began telling him what he had uncovered.

The Pope was not surprised and said, "Guy, as you know, De Noailles was selected by Louis, so it doesn't really surprise me that he and the King would like to rid me and place him on the throne of St. Peter's. It's been like that since my selection as the Head of the Church. So how do we take care of this?"

"Your Holiness," Guy started to say, "We can use this against Louis to make sure he comes to your terms. I am positive that he would want this to stay quiet, avoiding any public knowledge."

"Fine," the Pope answered, "But who might else be involved is my next question?"

Guy responded, "Niccolo and I suspect that the other Legates are involved somehow, and we will find out quickly enough. He will be following them like their shadows, and we will make sure this doesn't happen again. I, on the other hand, will follow the Cardinal to France and alert Louis of this deception. I am sure he will want to take care of this personally."

Guy went on. "I've instructed Niccolo to search the rooms of the Legates before they return tonight. He has taken one of the stable horses, which he will return in the morning. And should he find anything, he will let you know!"

"Alright," the Pope said, but both of you need to keep me informed, particularly with Louis."

"I will, Your Holiness," Guy responded and then said, "I bid you farewell and goodnight."

The Friar
Chapter Thirty-Seven

Leaving the Vatican, the Cardinal waited for the Legates, at the road that bends to his estate.

It wasn't too long after that the nervous and rather loud Legates appeared and were surprised at seeing the De Noailles standing against the stone column of Magdalen created by an unknown artist.

He said to the Legates, "Gentlemen, this is not the time or place to be speaking out loud of such matters. You must resume your normal daily lives as we plan out our next move to remove the Pope.

The Legates nodding their heads started to speak when the Cardinal continued.

"I will leave first thing in the morning and will contact you once I reach Paris. Let things calm down for now. You two must stay here until I notify you that it's time to put into place our next move. Got it?"

Hector replied for both and said, "I understand. I hope that Guy does not suspect us. And I am not sure now about that Niccolo. He seems to be awfully close to the Pontiff. He could be a spy?"

"Don't be silly," responded Angelo. "He's just a boy!"

De Noailles, laughed and said, "Yes, but is he working for the Pope. We must be careful. By the way, where is the poison that was used on Roberto? Did you remove it from your rooms?"

Angelo replied, "I left it in my room, but I will make sure that it is safely tucked away, in case we need to use it again."

"Alright," the Cardinal responded. "Make sure you return to your duties here and be alert. I will be in touch."

Outside the Inn, around midnight, Niccolo arrived on horseback that was now exhausted from being ridden so hard and fast.

Rushing inside, the Friar tried not to make a sound as he crept upstairs first into Angelo's room.

Through the moonlight, shining into the room, he was able to search every nook until he found a small drawer that wouldn't open.

Reaching underneath, Niccolo found a latch that released the lock, and the drawer sprung open into his palm. With one hand searching in the narrow felt lined drawer, he came across a tiny bottle. After extracting it, he saw that the bottle had a cork and a piece of cloth that was tied with twine.

Niccolo placed the bottle close to his nose without touching his skin, and he immediately moved his head backward. The smell was overwhelming. A poison of some sort, he was sure.

Wrapping the bottle into another cloth that he had in his pocket, Niccolo placed the drawer back into its proper position and exited the room.

Now walking towards Hector's room, Louise, with a candle in one hand, quietly approached Niccolo.

"What are you doing?" She asked.

Niccolo motioned with his finger on his lips and took her by her hand and opened the other Legates door, motioning for Louise to stay in the doorway.

Inside Hector's room, he found the same type of desk with a locked drawer that he was able to unlatch. Instead of finding more poison, he found a small book, and he placed it inside his tunic before reattaching the latch and sliding the drawer closed.

Out in the hallway, Niccolo whispered into Louise's ear that he would return shortly as he had to place the horse in the back stable. He didn't want to the Legates to know that he had gotten there before them and searched their rooms.

Half an hour later, Niccolo laid his tired body next to Louise's and just hugged her.

He whispered in her ear that he would tell her everything in the morning.

The Legates, having taken a carriage to the Inn, after meeting with De Noailles, stopped at a nearby tavern, where they proceeded to get very drunk.

Managing to close the tavern, they walked the rest of the way back to the Inn, and both Hector and Angelo went straight to bed without checking their desks.

The Friar
Chapter Thirty-Eight

In the morning after nursing their headaches and eating a small amount of breakfast, the Legates returned to their rooms and proceeded to unlock their desk drawers to find items missing.

At first, Hector ran to Angelo's room and almost cried out that his book was missing. And at the same time, Angelo said out loud, "Oh my God, the vile is missing too!"

Still at the morning table sat Louise and Niccolo, who were having a leisurely breakfast, when running towards them were the Legates out of breath.

Angelo was the first to speak. "Have you found anything lately Louise that did not belong to anyone else?"

"No," responded Louise.

Hector then said, "Well, have you recently cleaned our rooms?"

Again, Louise responded. "No, not since this past Monday. Since this is Friday, I would not have been in either of your rooms till today."

"Liar," Hector yelled.

Just then, Roberto came in and said, "What's all the yelling about?"

Hector, who was getting angrier by the minute, began accusing Louise of being a liar and thief.

Roberto, stunned by the outbreak from this holier than though man, asked Hector to quiet down.

Angelo then said, "Alright, alright. We are missing items of importance from our desks, and since you all are the only ones that maintain the Inn, we can only suspect you two of stealing our property."

Roberto was utterly shocked by being accused of such a thing and began to get excited himself, collapsed into a nearby chair.

Niccolo jumped up and yelled at the Legates.

He said, "Both of you need to stop. Unless you can prove that either Roberto or Louise had anything to do with it, then I would honestly ask you to pack your bags and move out as quickly as you can. "

The Friar continued, "If you do not, I will have the Vatican Guards come and remove you. Do you understand?"

Hector responded. "Who do you think you are? I knew you were in cahoots with the Pope! No problem, yes, we will move out this afternoon after we voice our concerns and discredit with this Inn."

Niccolo grabbed Hector, who was shorter, by the collar, and said, "You do that, Gentlemen. I am sure His Holiness will want to know what you two are missing and why you are accusing Roberto and Louise!"

The Friar
Chapter Thirty-Nine

After the Legates left Roberto's, they ended up near the Vatican in the area of Borgo. There the men found a place to eat that was close to another Inn owned by a French Italian patriot.

He was only too happy to receive the Papal messengers, even without knowing the reasons. It was all about the money as they paid the Innkeeper in advance.

Neither Hector, or Angelo noticed that Niccolo had followed them to Borgo.

Crossing the bridge to Castel Sant'Angelo, Niccolo sent a message to the Pope of what the latest developments were.

The Friar, through Cardinal Giacomo Antonio Moriggia, the Pope's secretary, notified His Holiness of his findings.

The information provided Clement included the vial of poison used and the book that had the names of the Electors from the prior Conclave.

De Noailles would have needed this list to determine who would vote for him to be the next Pope.

It also enclosed directions from Cardinal De Noailles regarding how much poison was to be poured into the cup of wine the Pope would drink from.

Niccolo requested troops from Cardinal Moriggia to detain the Legates and bring them to the Pope.

Following up on the message, Clement instructed Moriggia to comply with the Friar's request.

By nightfall, the two Legates had been placed under arrest and were now in custody at the Castel Sant'Angelo.

Returning to his room, Niccolo spent the night with Louise.

There in the moonlight, they both confessed their love for each other.

Then Niccolo told her that he was giving up his robe so that they could be together for the rest of their lives.

Louise was happy but fearful that Niccolo would regret this change in his life.

However, Niccolo said, "God had always taken care of me, even when I did not know. I am sure that he will take care of us and our endeavors to make a life together, and I will promise you that I will also work each day to provide a home for us."

Louise was forever happy that she found her true love, and as the two lovers looked into each other's eyes, there was nothing that could stop them now.

Days later, following the interrogation of the Legates, the Holy Father learned about the theft of the Head of St, John, and the detailed explanation of the poison used on Roberto.

Hector said to The Pope in person, "Your Holiness, it was never our intent to kill anyone. It was the Cardinal. He wanted to be Pope, and he had convinced us that it was the right thing to do."

Angelo then said, "Stealing the Head was also the Cardinal's idea. He said it would cause chaos between you and King Louis. Both of us ask your forgiveness in our misdirection's and request absolution in this matter."

The Pope stared past the two chained men, kneeling in front of him and replied.

"Gentlemen, I believed that both of you were honorable and trustworthy. It bothers and angers me that you would have been swayed in your paths. Whether a man wears a robe or not, common sense should have prevailed in knowing what evil deeds Cardinal De Noailles was presenting in front of you. For now, you must understand that my hands are tied. Guards, please remove the prisoners. I must think on this how I must punish them for these acts."

With that, the Guards made the two men stand up and escorted them out of the Raphael Room, back to Castel Sant Angelo.

The men never saw the outside world again. They both died before Clement and were buried in an unmarked grave outside of Rome.

The Friar
Chapter Forty

By the time the Cardinal had returned to Paris and his home, he had not been informed of the arrest of the Legates. He had believed that all was under control.

Meanwhile, Guy Benoit had already visited with the King and told him in detail what exactly took place in Rome.

Louis was appalled that such an act would take place, though he didn't rule out that the Cardinal would have attempted something so brazen and bizarre without the King's knowledge.

Guy said to the King, "I believe that the Legates were in cahoots with the Cardinal, and I am sure by now that the Pope's Guards have arrested them."

Louis sensing that he needed to coordinate a response with the Pope regarding all three men said to Guy, "Those men and the Cardinal should be jailed for their actions. In the interim, I will have the Cardinal arrested and interrogated for the truth. You must inform the Pope that I will do what I can, and I ask for his support in this matter.

However, I wish for the Pope to allow me *to* select the Bishops of France, and I will loosen my hold on the Protestants."

A month passed by, and the Pope and the King agreed over the matters of the three men and the compromises Clement and Louis would make. Cardinal De Noailles was to remain in the Bastille, for the rest of his life, while the Legates would be imprisoned in Rome.

Nothing else was ever said of either incident between Louis, or Clement.

The Friar
Chapter Forty-One

Following his assistance to the Pope, Niccolo resigned as a Friar, which is called Laicization. It is a term used in the loss of the clerical state.

Niccolo also requested dispensation from the Pope to marry Louise.

In the months and years after, Roberto passed away from natural causes.

Niccolo helped Louise run the Inn, as Roberto had deemed that she was his rightful heir in his will.

Though they planned to marry, it was only a short time after that, when Louise also passed away.

Following these calamities, years went by, as Niccolo spent his time managing the Vatican's Lodge, as it was now known, until the Pope's death.

Though Niccolo's one and only true love had died, he also lost his faith in the Church and stopped going to Mass.

However, Clement, being like his adopted father, would hold weekly meetings with Niccolo to try and convince him that it was alright to grieve for

Louise but that he needed to return to the cloth of the Church.

To no avail, Niccolo begged Clement to allow him to be.

Many times. in his apartment, the Pontiff would have deep arguments with Niccolo over God, Christ, and Death.

Then in March 1721, Pope Clement XI died at the age of 71.

Surrounding his death bed, were the Cardinals, several Bishops, two Doctors, his Altar Boys, and Niccolo, who sat in his worn-out clothes listening to the Pope's last words.

In his final moments, the Pope smiled at the now grown ex-Friar and placed his hand over Niccolo's and said, "It's time to come home!"

With that, the Pope died.

Niccolo held back the tears in his eyes, looking at his mentor.

Without much effort, Niccolo stood up and started walking out of the bedchamber.

As he began stepping down each of the 56 worn steps, Niccolo's mind traveled back and forth of his years he spent with the Pope.

Reaching the bottom, he walked past the Swiss Guards as they nodded to the Friar. His thoughts raced around his brain as he continued to walk across St Peter's Square.

To him, the day seemed brighter even with the clouds on that dark day. Niccolo knew it was a sign as the sunlight streaked across the sky.

Walking back, after changing, to where it all begun, Niccolo stepped into the Basilica of St Clemente's.

Now kneeling in his torn and tattered dirty white linen robe, so long ago forgotten, he made the sign of the cross.

Looking up at the altar, the Friar said a prayer.

"For all that I've done and accomplished, Dear Lord, I could not have done this without the Holy Father, Pope Clement. May he rest in peace, and may my days be fruitful being the Friar that he taught me to be."

The End.

www.ingramcontent.com/pod-product-compliance
Lightning Source LLC
Chambersburg PA
CBHW020615250626
47154CB00004B/1528